RANDOM HOUSE
CHILDREN'S BOOKS

TITLE:	Revenge of the Living Ted
AUTHOR:	Barry Hutchison
ILLUSTRATOR:	Lee Cosgrove
ILLUSTRATIONS:	Black-and-white illustrations throughout
IMPRINT:	Delacorte Press
PUBLICATION DATE:	September 8, 2020
ISBN:	978-0-593-17430-2
TENTATIVE PRICE:	$9.99 U.S./$13.99 CAN.
EBOOK ISBN:	978-0-593-17431-9
PAGES:	208
TRIM SIZE:	5-1/2" x 8-1/4"
AGES:	8–12

Please send any review or mention of this book to:
Random House Children's Books Publicity Department
1745 Broadway, Mail Drop 9-1
New York, NY 10019

rhkidspublicity@penguinrandomhouse.com

REVENGE OF THE LIVING TED

REVENGE OF THE LIVING TED

BARRY HUTCHISON ILLUSTRATED BY LEE COSGROVE

Delacorte Press

Text copyright © 2020 by Barry Hutchison
Jacket art copyright © 2020 by Lee Cosgrove

All rights reserved. Published in the United States by Delacorte Press, an imprint of Random House Children's Books, a division of Penguin Random House LLC, New York. Originally published in hardcover in the United States by Stripes Publishing, an imprint of the Little Tiger Group, in 2019.

Delacorte Press and the colophon are registered trademarks of Penguin Random House LLC.

Visit us on the Web! rhcbooks.com
Educators and librarians, for a variety of teaching tools,
visit us at RHTeachersLibrarians.com

Library of Congress Cataloging-in-Publication Data
tk

Printed in the United States of America

10 9 8 7 6 5 4 3 2 1

For Jessie and Bobby
—B.H.

For Freddie, Megan and Molly
—L.C.

Lisa Marie woke with a start from a bad dream, sat up suddenly and immediately headbutted her older brother.

THONK!

"Ow!" she said. Which, coincidentally, was exactly what her brother said.

"What did you do that for?" Vernon demanded, rubbing the spot on his forehead where Lisa Marie had clonked him.

"I didn't do it on purpose!" Lisa Marie retorted. She looked around at her neat and tidy bedroom. "Why are you in my room? What were you doing leaning over me? Were you going to shout in my ear to wake me up?"

Vernon looked hurt. "I can't believe you think I'd do that to you!"

"You do it at least once a week," Lisa Marie pointed out.

Vernon smirked. "Oh. Yeah. So I do." The smirk became a full-blown grin. "Okay, you got me."

Lisa Marie shuffled back so she was sitting upright in bed. She yawned, stretched and studied her stepbrother. "Are you okay?" she asked.

"I think so," said Vernon. "But it might leave a lump."

"Not your head," Lisa Marie said. "I mean, are you okay after last night?"

Vernon blinked. "What? Why, what happened last night?"

"The . . . You know, the . . . I mean . . ." Lisa Marie's voice became a shrill whisper. "What do you mean, 'What happened last night?' The teddy bears! You don't remember?"

Vernon raised one eyebrow. "Teddy bears? I don't know what you're talking about," he said.

Lisa Marie gasped. "What?! But—"

Vernon's face split into a grin. "Sorry, couldn't resist. You should see your face," he laughed. "Yes, I remember."

He shivered, recalling the army of evil teddy bears that had almost been the end of both of them. "How could I forget something like that?"

Lisa Marie relaxed. "And you're okay?"

Vernon nodded. "Think so, yeah. I mean, it was all a bit . . ."

"Discombobulating?" Lisa Marie guessed. Big words were one of her favorite things, and *discombobulating* was one of her favorite big words.

"I have no idea what that means," Vernon admitted.

"It sort of means 'disconcerting,'" Lisa Marie explained.

Vernon continued to look at her.

Lisa Marie sighed. "Confusing."

"Right. Gotcha. Couldn't you just have said that in the first place?" asked Vernon. "I was going to say 'terrifying,' but yeah, it was disco bobbing or whatever too."

Lisa Marie didn't bother trying to correct him.

He was probably saying it wrong on purpose to annoy her.

"And yes, I'm fine," Vernon said. "You?"

Lisa Marie reached for her glasses, which were sitting on her bedside table. She pulled them on, then nodded. "I'm okay," she confirmed.

And she was. It was surprising how okay she was, really. She'd been woken up just after midnight last night by Henrietta, the witch bear she'd made at the Create-a-Ted shop, and had watched helplessly as her dad and stepmom had been turned into a frog and a slug.

From there things had quickly gotten even worse, thanks to Vernon's demon-vampire-werewolf bear, Grizz, and his army of evil teds. Luckily, Lisa Marie, Vernon and a very special teddy named Bearvis had worked together to stop Grizz's evil plan. They'd definitely saved the town and probably the whole world.

It was a good thing it had been a Friday night so she didn't have to get up early next morning for . . .

She sat forward suddenly in bed.

THONK!

"Ow! Will you stop doing that?" Vernon yelped, rubbing his forehead again.

"It's Saturday!" Lisa Marie said. "Morning. It's Saturday morning!"

"And that's a good reason to headbutt me?"

"It's the first. It's the first of November!"

Vernon began to frown, but his eyebrows worked out what Lisa Marie meant before his brain did and quickly went into reverse.

"Yeah. What's . . . ?" He gasped. "Dad's birthday! I mean *your* dad's birthday. I mean Steve's birthday! I mean—"

"I know what you mean!" Lisa Marie told him. She threw back her covers and swung her legs out of bed, forcing Vernon to jump to his feet. "Let's go and wish him a happy birthday."

Vernon nodded. "Okay," he said. Then he chewed his lip. "Think he remembers being a frog?"

"Not sure," Lisa Marie admitted, taking her

bathrobe off the back of her door. "Think Mom remembers being a slug?"

Vernon puffed out his cheeks. "Dunno," he said. "But I guess there's only one way to find out."

Lisa Marie had many impressive skills—knowing science facts off the top of her head, solving crossword puzzles and saving the world from evil stuffed toys, to name but three. Singing, however, was not one of them.

She stood in the middle of the living room, screeching her way through "Happy Birthday," while Vernon mumbled halfheartedly along with her. As they reached the "dear Daaaaa-aaaaaad" part, Lisa Marie's voice almost shattered the lightbulb, and forced Vernon to plug his ears with his pinkie fingers.

When the song was finally over, Lisa Marie

threw her arms around her dad's waist, then presented him with the card she had made.

Because she was almost as bad at art as she was at singing, she'd decided to cut letters out of a magazine to spell out the message on the front. It had seemed like a good idea at the time, but as she handed it over she couldn't help but feel it looked like something a kidnapper might send to demand a ransom.

"Thank you, sweetheart. It's very creative," Dad said, setting the card in pride of place on the mantelpiece.

Vernon snorted. "How much do they want for the hostages, Steve?" he asked. "And where are you supposed to leave the money?"

Vernon's mom—Lisa Marie's stepmom—shot Vernon a playfully stern look. "I suppose your card is a work of art, is it?" she asked.

"Uh, I didn't make a card," Vernon said. "But we did get you a present! And I helped pay for it, even though we could've got you one for free."

Dad looked a little confused. "Uh, okay. Thanks?"

"Don't mention it," said Vernon.

Lisa Marie opened the living-room cupboard and pulled out a box. It was quite a bashed and battered box, with several tears in the wrapping paper that had been clumsily taped back together. She clutched it to her chest for a moment, like she didn't really want to hand it over.

"Am I getting it, then?" Dad asked.

"Yep," said Lisa Marie, but she kept hugging the box.

Dad smiled. "When? Next birthday?" he teased.

Forcing her fingers to release their grip, Lisa Marie reluctantly passed the box to her dad. He noticed the damaged wrapping for the first time and eyed the package warily.

"Happy birthday," Lisa Marie said. "Again. I hope you like it."

"I'm sure I'll love it," Dad replied, looking just a little nervous as he tugged on the torn wrapping paper. His eyes grew wider when he saw the clear plastic window of the box inside.

"No!" he gasped. "You didn't?"

Staring out from inside the box was a teddy bear. Not just any teddy bear, though. It was a bear styled on Dad's all-time favorite singer, Elvis Presley.

"Elvis!" Dad laughed.

"Technically, his name's Bearvis," said Lisa Marie. "The shop wasn't allowed to call him Elvis."

"For legal reasons," Vernon said. He shrugged. "Or so the shop guy said."

"But anyway, he prefers to be called the King," Lisa Marie concluded.

Dad chuckled. "I bet he does!"

Prying open the box lid, he pulled the teddy bear out. It wore a white jumpsuit and matching cape, both of which were covered in shiny sequins. His hair was sleek black and teased up into an impressive pompadour.

At least, that's how he was *supposed* to look. In reality, his outfit was quite badly stained with dirt and soot, and there was a perfectly round hole through his hair, as if someone had shot at it with a ray gun.

Which, coincidentally, was exactly what had happened.

"He looks a bit like he's been dragged backward through a bush," Dad observed.

Which, again, was exactly what had happened.

"Does he?" said Lisa Marie, taking the teddy and examining it. His eyes stared glassily back at her—it was hard to imagine that just a few hours ago he'd been fighting heroically at her side. "Oh, you're right. That's a shame. I'd better hold on to him, in that case."

She tucked Bearvis under her arm. "We'll get you something else."

"No, it's—"

Lisa Marie held up a hand to silence him. "Dad, please. I couldn't possibly ask you to accept a present that's in such bad condition. I'll keep him. We'll get you something else."

"Flies," said Vernon.

Everyone looked at him.

"Sorry?" asked Dad.

Vernon narrowed his eyes and studied his stepdad's reaction. "We could get you some flies. You know, to eat?"

"Why would I want to eat flies?"

"I don't know. You tell me," said Vernon. "Why *do* you want to eat flies?"

"He doesn't!" said Mom. She looked at her husband. "You don't, do you?"

"Not that I know of."

Vernon nodded. "Interesting," he said. "So, on a scale of one to ten, how much do you feel like a frog?"

"What are you doing?" Lisa Marie whispered.

"Can it be a scale of *zero* to ten?" Dad asked.

"Okay," Vernon said.

"Zero. I feel zero out of ten like a frog."

Vernon nodded again. *"Interesting."* He shrugged. "Fair enough, then."

Before he could ask his mom how much, on a scale of one to ten, she felt like a slug, Lisa Marie jumped in. "So, um, anything interesting on the news this morning?"

"Not really," said Dad. "Obviously all the news anchors got together to wish me a happy birthday, but other than that it was just the usual."

"Nothing . . . odd?" said Lisa Marie.

Mom frowned. "Like what?"

"Oh, I don't know," Lisa Marie said, twirling her hair and trying to look innocent. "Just anything unusual or out of the ordinary."

"Like a load of teddy bears coming to life and trying to take over the town," said Vernon. He blushed slightly when everyone stared at him again. "You know, just as an example."

Mom and Dad exchanged a glance. "No," said Mom. "I think we'd have noticed that."

This time, it was Lisa Marie's turn to say, "Interesting."

She jabbed a thumb in the direction of the door. "Anyway, we're just going to go get you a new present."

"The bear's fine," said Dad. "Honest."

"No! I'm keeping him!" said Lisa Marie, hugging the glassy-eyed ted tighter. She smiled sweetly. "I mean, we'll find you something else. Come on, Vernon."

Vernon blinked in surprise, then trotted after her toward the front door. It was only once she'd pulled it open that her dad stopped her.

"Uh, you should probably get dressed and have breakfast first."

Lisa Marie looked down at her pajamas and

bathrobe. She'd saved the world wearing not much more, but she couldn't exactly tell her parents that.

"Yes," she said, closing the door again. "I probably should."

Lisa Marie and Vernon strolled side by side toward the town center, Bearvis tucked under Lisa Marie's arm. She felt bad taking back the present, but after everything she and Bearvis had been through, she couldn't stand the thought of anyone else having him, even Dad.

The street seemed so . . . normal, with people going about their business as if nothing had happened. It was hard to believe that just a few hours ago the children had been fighting for their lives here.

"It's good my mom and your dad don't remember anything," said Vernon.

"You could just call them Mom and Dad you know?" Lisa Marie replied. "And yes, it's good."

She looked around at the people on the street. A woman jogged by, all red-faced and sweaty. A man pushed a double stroller with two toddlers securely strapped within. He yawned as he passed, his eyes barely open.

"It's kind of weird, though, isn't it?" Lisa Marie whispered. "The way everyone's acting like nothing happened."

Vernon shrugged. "Maybe they slept through it all."

Lisa Marie shook her head. "Grizz—the monster *you* created—took loads of people prisoner, remember? Word should have spread by now. There should be police and news cameras all over the place."

A man in a neon hoodie appeared around a corner ahead. He was tall, and stooped from the weight of the four shopping bags he was carrying. Lisa Marie gave Vernon a nudge.

"Look! That's what's-his-name."

"So?"

"So, he was one of the prisoners last night. Grizz—the monster *you* created—"

"You don't have to keep saying that."

"Well, I'm going to," Lisa Marie replied. "Grizz—the monster *you* created—had him tied up in the square with everyone else. He *must* remember."

Vernon looked the approaching what's-his-name up and down. "Maybe he doesn't want to talk about it. He might be a very private person, which is why we have no idea what his name is."

Lisa Marie started walking more quickly. "I'm going to ask him."

"What? No!" Vernon hissed, but he was too late. Lisa Marie beamed broadly as she approached what's-his-name.

"Good morning!" she said, blocking the man's path.

What's-his-name looked up and shuffled to a stop. "Uh, hi."

"My brother and I were just wondering if you had a good night last night," Lisa Marie said.

The man frowned and raised his eyes to Vernon as he ran up to join Lisa Marie.

"Huh?"

"Ignore her," said Vernon, but Lisa Marie persevered.

"We're doing a survey. For school."

"But it's Saturday."

"We're very dedicated students," Lisa Marie said. "Question one: What would you say was the most interesting thing that happened to you last night?"

What's-his-name sighed and adjusted his grip on the bags. "I don't know," he said. "We just watched a movie, really."

Lisa Marie clicked her tongue against the back of her teeth. "So, you weren't, say, abducted by monsters? Or teddy bears? Or monster teddy bears?"

The man snorted. 'Is this a joke? These bags are heavy, you know."

Vernon put his hands on Lisa Marie's shoulders and led her away. "Thanks for your time," he called back. "Very helpful."

"But—" Lisa Marie began.

"Shhh," Vernon whispered. "You can't just go around asking stuff like that. People are going to think you're a weirdo." He stopped. "Wait. What am I saying? You *are* a weirdo."

"There's nothing wrong with being different," Lisa Marie sniffed. "But what about what's-his-name? Don't you think *that's* weird? Either he's lying, or he doesn't remember what happened." She stroked Bearvis's head, deep in thought. "I could understand Mom and Dad not remembering—they weren't themselves—but what if *everyone's* forgotten? What if we're the only ones who know what happened?"

Vernon's forehead furrowed. Lisa Marie knew this meant he was thinking hard. She could almost hear the cogs creaking inside his head. "I know someone who's bound to remember," he eventually said.

"Of course!" Lisa Marie yelped. "Drake!"

Grabbing Vernon by the wrist, she checked for traffic, then crossed the road. "Let's go and see him," she said.

Vernon groaned. "I have a bad feeling about this," he muttered, but he didn't resist as Lisa Marie led him to Drake's street.

Neither of the children noticed the sleek black car with darkened windows that had been following them since they left the house. They didn't hear its engine purr as it crept along the road behind them, or see the beady eyes watching them from behind the tinted glass.

It was pretty rare for Vernon to have good ideas, but going to Drake's house was definitely one of them, Lisa Marie thought. If anyone would remember the battle of the living teddy bears, it was Drake. He did get turned into one, after all. When they'd last seen him, he'd been barely a foot tall, covered in fur and wearing an adorable little bow. That wasn't something he was likely to forget in a hurry.

Lisa Marie felt a little guilty as they approached Drake's house. He was a nasty bully, but even he didn't deserve to be stuck as a teddy bear. She should have done more to try to turn him back to his normal horrible self.

The front yard was full of cheerful-looking gnomes with colorful hats and bushy beards. Lisa Marie scanned their faces to make sure none of them was a teddy bear version of Drake in disguise, then led Vernon up the path to the front door.

"What are we going to say?" he whispered. "What if his mom answers?"

"We'll just ask her if Drake's in," Lisa Marie replied.

"And what if she says, 'Yes, but he's a teddy bear'? What then?"

Lisa Marie shrugged. "We'll cross that bridge when we come to it."

She stopped on the front step and rang the doorbell. Vernon danced anxiously behind her like he was desperate for a bathroom. Even when he wasn't an angry teddy bear, Drake made him nervous.

"This is a bad idea," he whispered. Then he stopped dancing and stood to attention as the door opened.

Drake's mom stood just inside the doorway, smiling warmly. She wore a fluffy pink bathrobe with a unicorn pattern on it that Lisa Marie very much approved of. She smiled at Vernon, vaguely recognizing him, then looked down at Lisa Marie as she spoke.

"Good morning. We'd like to speak to Drake, please," Lisa Marie announced.

Drake's mom looked a little taken aback by Lisa Marie's confidence. "Well, okay," she replied, still smiling. "Are you sure, though? He's not exactly at his most charming in the morning."

Lisa Marie didn't imagine there was any time of day when Drake could be considered charming.

"Yes, please."

"Okay. Good luck!" Drake's mom said. She turned and called back into the house. "Wakey-wakey, Drakey-Drakey!"

From somewhere upstairs there came a sleepy moan. "Ugh. What time is it?"

Vernon let out a nervous whimper. That was Drake's voice, and he didn't sound happy.

"It's time to come to the door, that's what time. Your friends are here to see you," his mom replied. She winked at Lisa Marie and smiled. "Boys," she said.

23

"Tell me about it," Lisa Marie sighed. She jabbed a thumb in Vernon's direction. "You should try living with this one."

"No thanks. One's bad enough!"

Vernon cleared his throat. "Have you *seen* Drake?"

"Uh, yes. He's my son," Drake's mom replied, looking a little confused by the question.

"What? Oh. No. I mean have you seen him this morning?" Vernon asked.

"Ah. No. Not yet." There was a thudding of footsteps behind her. "But this sounds like his dainty feet now."

She gave the children a little wave, then stepped aside just as Drake appeared. Half of his hair was standing on end, and there was some dried drool on his cheek. One of his eyes was stuck shut with sleep, while the other glared pure hatred at them.

Lisa Marie and Vernon noticed all of these things. The thing they noticed most of all, though, was that he definitely was not a teddy bear.

"What?" he demanded. "What are you two

doing here? If you've come to get your Halloween candy back, you're too late. I already ate it."

"You're human again," Lisa Marie said.

"What do you mean 'again'?" Drake snapped.

"You're not a teddy bear," Lisa Marie continued.

Drake blinked a few times until both eyes were

open, then scowled at Vernon. "What's the little freak talking about?"

Vernon tried frantically to come up with an explanation. "It's, uh, it was a dare. She was dared to come and ask if you were a teddy bear."

There was a long pause as Drake thought about this. "Dared by who?"

Vernon's mouth went dry as Drake glared at him. His mind raced as he tried to think of someone. He glanced back over his shoulder and caught a glimpse of a gnome's pointy red hat.

"Santa," he blurted. He bit his lip, immediately regretting this answer.

Drake's eyes narrowed. "Santa?"

"Mr. Santa," Vernon babbled. "He's our neighbor. Old Mr. Santa. You probably don't know him."

Lisa rolled her eyes and muttered quietly below her breath. "Well, this is embarrassing." She caught Vernon by the arm. "Come on, we'd better go."

"Yeah, you'd better," Drake growled after them. He fixed Vernon with another of his glares. "And don't forget the tournament later."

Vernon frowned. "Tournament?"

"I *knew* you'd forget," Drake growled. "The multiplayer tournament. On Xbox? *Battle War Two.*"

"Oh. Yeah. Right! Didn't forget," said Vernon.

"Just be online. We're top of the leaderboard, and if you mess it up . . . ," Drake barked.

"I won't mess it up!" Vernon insisted. "I'll be online."

"You'd better be," Drake hissed. He turned away and began to close the door. Lisa Marie and Vernon both gasped as they spotted an adorable pink bow tangled in the hair at the back of his head. It was the same bow he'd worn when he'd been transformed into a teddy.

"Drake!" Lisa Marie cried.

Drake scowled at her. "What now?"

Lisa Marie opened her mouth to tell him about the bow, then changed her mind. "Nothing. Have a nice day."

With a grunt, Drake slammed the door. Lisa Marie and Vernon retreated along the path and out onto the street.

"Mr. Santa?" Lisa Marie asked with a smirk.

Vernon scowled. "Shut up. It was the best I could do."

"Yeah. That's what worries me," Lisa Marie giggled. She glanced back at Drake's front door. "He's not a bear."

"No."

"He doesn't even remember being a bear."

"Doesn't look like it, no."

"It doesn't make sense!" Lisa Marie protested. "It's completely illogical. Why does nobody remember?"

Vernon shrugged. "I don't know. Maybe it was a dream."

"Don't be ridiculous," Lisa Marie said.

Vernon threw up his arms in a shrug. "What's more ridiculous? That it was a dream, or that a magic machine brought a load of teddy bears to life, and that they then attempted to take over the town?"

Lisa Marie began to list things on her fingers. "Okay, one, if it was a dream, then it would mean we both had *exactly* the same dream. Which is impossible."

"So is teddy bears coming to life."

"*Two,*" continued Lisa Marie, ignoring him. She held up Bearvis. "He's covered in dirt and someone shot a hole through his hair. Why?"

"Because it's stupid hair?" Vernon guessed.

"Because he was alive," said Lisa Marie. She hugged Bearvis again. "And it's beautiful hair."

She went back to counting on her fingers. "And three . . . Well, I don't need a three, because the first two were so conclusive. The teddy bears came to life, Vernon. It happened, and somehow we're the only ones who remember. It's all so . . ."

Vernon groaned. "Don't say it."

"Discombobulating," said Lisa Marie. She lowered her voice to a whisper. "Someone must have made everyone forget. It's the only explanation. The question is—who?"

Vernon shrugged. "I guess we'll never know," he said.

As the words left his mouth, black cloth bags were pulled over both children's heads from behind and two pairs of rough, furry hands bundled them into the back of a car.

"Hey! What's going on?" Vernon yelped.

"Let us go!" Lisa Marie cried.

There was a hiss from somewhere inside the car. Lisa Marie tasted something bitter at the back of her throat.

"Gas," she coughed, her voice becoming slurred. "It's sleeping g—"

And then she slumped sideways in her seat and Vernon flopped down on top of her.

Vernon jumped awake with a high-pitched "Yeuragh!" He karate-chopped the air for a few frantic moments, then realized there was nobody around worth karate-chopping.

He was sitting at an impressively long wooden table that had been polished to a mirrorlike sheen. Lisa Marie sat across from him, wide awake. She still held Bearvis under one arm, like she was trying to keep him safe.

"Ugh. My mouth tastes like feet," Vernon croaked.

Lisa Marie motioned to a jug of water that had been placed between them. "You could have a drink," she said.

Vernon reached for a glass.

"But it might be poisoned."

Vernon stopped reaching for a glass and sat back.

"Where are we?" he grunted, peeling his eyes all the way open and looking around. They were in a long room with an expensive-looking carpet and lots of certificates hanging on the wall in fancy frames.

Vernon squinted at the closest one and tried to read the ornate writing.

"It's for businessman of the year," Lisa Marie said. "I've already read them."

"How long have you been awake?" Vernon asked.

"Longer than you," Lisa Marie replied. "And I've come to a few conclusions. Firstly, we're in the boardroom of a large and successful business. Secondly, we're here because somebody used sleeping gas on us and bundled us into a car. Although not in that order."

"Right! I remember that!" said Vernon, rubbing his head.

"Thirdly," continued Lisa Marie. She moved her feet under the table. A set of chains around her ankles rattled noisily. "I think we're in trouble."

Vernon looked down at his own feet. He too was tethered to the floor by some impressively heavy chains.

"We're chained up!" he said.

"Yes."

"We're chained up!"

Lisa Marie nodded. "Yes. I know. We've established that."

Vernon's face had turned pale. His eyes were so wide they looked like they might be about to fall out onto the table. "Why are we chained up?"

"That I don't know," Lisa Marie admitted.

Vernon fumbled in his pocket. "I'll phone for help," he said, taking out his mobile. He tapped the screen, then stared at it in horror. "No signal!"

"Yes, it's the thick roof, you see? It blocks the transmissions," boomed a voice from the far end of the boardroom. The door stood wide open, revealing the most ludicrously shaped human being Lisa Marie had ever seen.

He wasn't particularly tall, but his upper body was almost impossibly wide. It wasn't that he was fat, exactly; it was more like he was the *exact opposite* of thin. His broad shoulders led down to a barrel chest, then on to hips that wouldn't have looked out of place on a baby elephant.

His legs, in contrast, grew gradually skinnier the farther down they went. His hefty thighs became slender calves, followed by a pair of tiny feet. In silhouette, he looked a bit like an ice cream cone.

The sight of him made Lisa Marie nervous, but she was determined not to show it. "Who are you?" she demanded.

The man wobbled forward, leaning on a cane to take some of the weight off his legs. As he stepped into the boardroom the shadows fell away, giving Lisa Marie and Vernon a better look at him.

He wore a neatly pressed pair of trousers, shiny shoes and a shirt so white it seemed to glow. The shirt's sleeves had been rolled up, revealing two of the thickest and hairiest arms the children had ever seen.

The hair didn't stop there. His face was mostly covered by a coarse black beard, which sprouted in every direction at once. Between the beard and his enormously bushy eyebrows, there was very little of the man's actual face visible other than a forehead, a glimpse of cheeks, and two eyes that stared out from the tangled jungle of hair.

"My name is Ursine Kodiak," he said. His voice

was loud and rumbled like thunder. Teeth appeared inside his beard. Lisa Marie hoped he was smiling. "And I'm about to change your lives forever."

There was one other chair positioned at the far end of the table. It groaned in protest as Ursine lowered himself into it. He held on to the table for a moment, as if worried the chair might collapse, but then nodded and relaxed farther into it.

"It seems you had an interesting evening yesterday," Ursine said.

"What do you want?" Vernon asked. He was even more nervous than Lisa Marie, but just like her, he was determined not to show it. "You have to let us go. Our parents will have called the police by now."

Ursine tilted his head from side to side, as if weighing Vernon's words. "Not yet. I have them under surveillance. They still think you're shopping. Even when they do get worried, there's nothing to connect me with your disappearance. I could keep you here for weeks if I wanted."

He leaned forward and glowered at Vernon. "So you see, I don't *have* to let you go at all."

Vernon gulped but didn't reply. He shot Lisa Marie a worried look. She was trying not to look scared, but he could see right through the act.

"But I will," Ursine said, smiling again. "Because I'm nice like that. I'm not holding you here against your will."

Lisa Marie rattled the chains around her ankles.

"Okay, maybe a tiny bit against your will," Ursine admitted. "But I just want to show you something. Then I'll make you an offer. If you choose to accept it, great. If not, you will be free to go."

"Then why go to the trouble of kidnapping us?" Lisa Marie asked. "Why not just ask us?"

Ursine rolled his eyes. "Yes. Sorry about that. It wasn't ideal, but my employees can't risk revealing themselves for too long in public, you see?"

He clapped his enormous hands twice, making Vernon jump.

"Cuddlyplump! Mr. Flufftton!" he boomed.

Two much smaller figures appeared in the doorway behind him, half hidden by shadow.

They both tried to get through the opening at the same time, got wedged there for a moment, then tumbled into the room as a ball of arms, legs and fur.

"Get off!"

"You get off!"

The new arrivals jumped to their feet, slapping at each other angrily.

"Enough!" boomed Ursine, which made them stop fighting. They scurried to either side of Ursine's chair and stood to attention. Only their heads were visible over the top of the table, but that was more than enough for the children to be able to work out what they were.

"Teddies," Lisa Marie gasped. "They're big teddies."

There was a *thonk* from across the table as Vernon flopped onto it face-first.

Ursine raised a caterpillar eyebrow. "Your brother seems to have fainted."

"Yes, he does that sometimes," Lisa Marie said. "He'll be okay in a minute."

Ursine clicked his tongue against his teeth. "Should we wait for him?"

"We probably should, if you don't mind," said Lisa Marie. "Or we'll have to explain everything again when he wakes up."

Ursine sighed. "Fine. We'll wait."

They waited. Ursine tapped a fingernail on the table, making a *tick-tick-tick* sound that echoed around the room.

Lisa Marie tried smiling at the two teddy bears, but neither of them smiled back.

Ursine puffed out his hairy cheeks. He hummed quietly below his breath for a while, then nodded at the bear under Lisa Marie's arm.

"You brought your friend, I see."

Lisa Marie tightened her grip on Bearvis. "Yes."

"He was impressive last night. Most impressive," Ursine said. He held out a hand. "May I see him?"

Lisa Marie shook her head. "No."

Ursine's beard twitched, revealing his teeth again. He was smiling. At least, Lisa Marie thought so. "Later, perhaps."

Lisa Marie quietly cleared her throat and nodded in Vernon's direction. "Shouldn't be long now," she said.

As if on cue, Vernon jumped awake. Screaming, he karate-chopped the air again for a few seconds, then caught Lisa Marie's look of disapproval. He lowered his arms, trying very hard not to blush.

"Must've been the effects of the sleeping gas," he said.

"Must have been," agreed Lisa Marie, although she didn't really believe it. She turned to Ursine. "Now, you were saying?"

40

"Hmm? Oh. Yes. I'm sure you've already worked out that I was the one responsible for your little . . . adventure last night."

Vernon looked across the table to his stepsister. "Had we worked that out?"

Lisa Marie nodded.

"I thought it was the shopkeeper guy?"

"Pah! That imbecile?" scoffed Ursine. He let out an animal-like snort. "I let him steal an early prototype of my . . ." He waved a hairy hand as if searching for the correct word. "*Contraption.* I wanted to see what would happen if it was activated out there in the real world."

"Monsters, that's what happened!" Vernon said. "Horrible teddy bear monsters."

Ursine's teeth appeared in his beard again as he grinned. "Yes. Fascinating. I was able to gather such useful data."

"How did you do it?" asked Lisa Marie. "How did you build a machine that could bring teddy bears to life?"

"Because I'm a genius, that's how!" Ursine crowed. "Also, my mother was a Nobel

41

Prize–winning physicist, and my father was a he-witch, so that helped."

"A he-witch?" said Vernon. "You mean a wizard?"

"Pah! Don't be ludicrous. There are no such thing as wizards. He was a he-witch."

Vernon stared blankly at the odd-shaped man for a moment, then shrugged. "Fair enough."

Lisa Marie leaned in Ursine's direction. He was still a long way down the table, so it didn't really have the menacing effect she'd been aiming for. "You wiped everyone's memories, didn't you? You made it so no one would remember."

Ursine nodded. "I felt it best to cover my tracks," he said. He stroked the heads of both teddy bear henchmen. They continued to stare at Lisa Marie and Vernon. "Of course, that was the easy part. The difficult bit was ensuring you two both remembered everything."

Lisa Marie glanced across the table at Vernon. "Why?" she asked. "Why did you want us to remember?"

"Because . . ."

Ursine stopped talking and stood up.

"In fact, no. I'm not going to tell you. I'll show you instead," he said.

With a whistle from their master, the two teddies scurried under the table and removed the chains from around the children's ankles.

"Now, if you will both follow me," Ursine said. Something wicked glinted in his eyes as he gestured to the door. "I'm about to blow your tiny minds."

Vernon let out a whimper. "What?!"

"It's a figure of speech," Lisa Marie assured him. She turned away and dropped her voice to a whisper. "I hope."

Lisa Marie and Vernon stood on a high metal walkway near the ceiling, gazing down into what seemed to be an enormous factory. Vernon was gripping the railing so tightly his knuckles had turned white.

"It's . . . It's . . . ," Lisa Marie began, but she stopped there. Despite her love of big words, she couldn't think of one that would even start to describe what was going on below.

"High!" Vernon squeaked. "It's *very* high!"

Lisa Marie tutted but couldn't really argue. It was *definitely* high.

Below them several vast machines, manned by an army of bears, filled the factory floor. They whirred and chugged and clunked as they worked to turn stacks of stuffing and fur into teddy bears. Lots of teddy bears. More teddy bears than Lisa Marie could even guess at, let alone count.

Like the two bears standing on the walkway behind them—Cuddlyplump and Mr. Fluffton— the teddies down on the factory floor were larger than normal. They were a little over half of Lisa Marie's height and around three times the size of Bearvis.

A series of conveyor belts linked all the machines. The raw materials for the bears were lowered onto three different belts at the start—one for stuffing, one for fur and a third for the eyes and plastic noses. They trundled through the network of machines, before feeding into the largest one at the end.

When the conveyor belt carried them out of that final machine, the bears were complete. They sat limp and motionless, their glassy eyes gazing blindly ahead.

Occasionally, a light on the machine would flash red and the conveyor belt would pause for

a second. When it started up again, there was always a gap where a bear should have been.

"Those are the duds," Ursine explained. "I have very strict quality control standards. Any bear that isn't *exactly* right gets rejected by the machine and dropped down the chute."

Lisa Marie hugged Bearvis. "What happens to them then?"

Ursine hesitated. "Do you know, I'm not really sure? They just gather dust, I suppose."

He gestured down at his factory. "So, what do you think?"

"I think I'd like to get d-down," Vernon squeaked.

"I think that's a lot of teddy bears," said Lisa Marie.

Ursine grunted. "Seriously? That's the best you can do? I thought you were supposed to be clever." He nodded to Vernon. "Well, not so much him."

"Hey!"

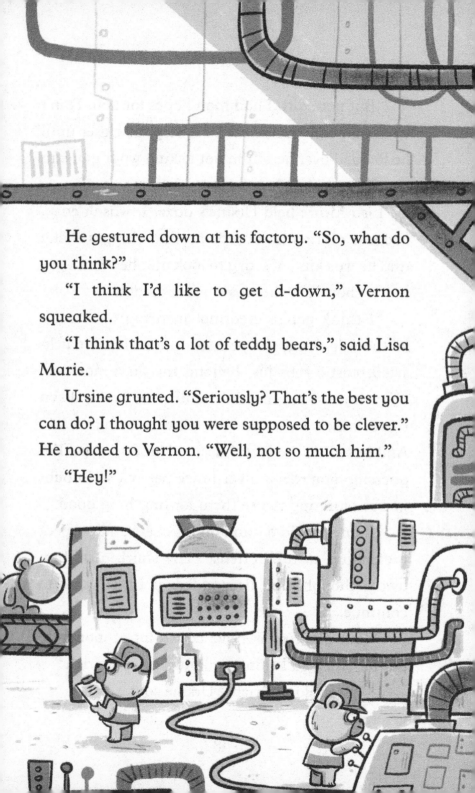

"But you, girl. I had high hopes for you. Don't let me down," Ursine said. He stepped closer until he loomed over her. "I'm not asking what you can see, I'm asking what do you *think*."

Lisa Marie held Ursine's gaze. It wasn't easy, because all that hair made finding his eyes tricky and he was kind of scary to look at. She wasn't going to show him she was afraid, though.

"I think you're creating an army," she said. Without looking, she pointed to a series of truck-sized plastic tubs just beyond the final machine. "You have a substantial number of bears down there, which I assume you plan to bring to life. And based on the fact that you kidnapped us, I'm guessing you're not a very nice person, so I doubt you're planning to use them for anything good."

Ursine placed a hand on his chest and gasped, pretending to take offense. His smirk gave him away, though, and he nodded at Lisa Marie to continue.

"This place must have cost a lot of money to put together, so I think you must be quite rich."

"I'm fabulously rich," Ursine said.

"Which means you aren't planning to use the bears to rob people. You don't want money."

Ursine raised his hairy eyebrows. "So . . . ?"

Lisa Marie clicked her tongue against the roof of her mouth. "So if I had to guess . . ."

"You do."

"I'd say you want power. You're planning to take over the world."

"Yes!" Ursine cheered. "I knew you were a smart one! I knew you'd figure it out! Bravo, girl, bravo!"

"I knew all that!" Vernon said. "Totally knew that's what was happening."

Lisa Marie knew that wasn't true and that Vernon was only trying to sound clever. She felt quite pleased with herself for managing to work everything out.

Well, *almost* everything.

"Why do you need us?" she wondered. "Why not wipe our memories too?"

"All in good time," Ursine said. He tilted his head back so he was looking at the ceiling. "Down," he commanded. He and the teddies grabbed hold of the railing, so Lisa Marie quickly did the same.

Vernon screamed as the walkway plunged toward the distant factory floor. He gripped the railing so hard the whiteness of his knuckles spread through his hand and up past his elbows.

He was still screaming when the walkway jerked to a stop just a few inches above the factory's concrete floor. Part of the railing swung open like a gate, and Ursine motioned for Lisa Marie to go through.

"Shall we?"

Before Lisa Marie could move, one of Ursine's teddy bear accomplices—the shorter of the two, whose fur was a lighter shade of brown than the other—gave her a shove from behind.

"Now, now, Mr. Fluffton," said Ursine. "Not so rough with our guest, please."

"Sorry, boss," Mr. Fluffton replied in a surprisingly gruff voice. He sounded like a gangster from an old movie.

The other bear pushed Vernon through the gate next, making him stumble and fall. Ursine didn't seem to have a problem with that.

"Hey! Guest, remember?" Vernon protested.

"Shut up, kid," snarled the darker-furred Cuddlyplump. He punched a clenched paw into the opposite palm in a way that was eighty percent threatening, twenty percent just too cute for words.

Lisa Marie helped Vernon up and they stood close together as Ursine and his hench-bears stepped down from the walkway. Ursine's cane clacked on the concrete as he led the way across the factory floor.

"This way. There's something else I want to show you."

Lisa Marie glanced down at Bearvis under her arm. His eyes stared blankly at the rows of towering machines as they passed between them. Lisa Marie wished, not for the first time, that he would spring to life like he had the night before.

The factory was much noisier down here, and the teddy bears it was producing loomed even larger up close. The machine that was putting their faces on had arranged the features into angry scowls. They were probably supposed to look scary, but Lisa Marie found them adorable.

There was a large screen fixed to one of the walls. The angle had made it impossible to see from up on the walkway, but now it was hard to miss. A single black eye stared out from the screen, sweeping left and right as if on the lookout for trouble.

Lisa Marie felt a shiver travel the length of her spine. "What's that?" she asked.

"That's Mommy Bear," said Ursine. "She's an artificial intelligence who keeps an eye on things around here."

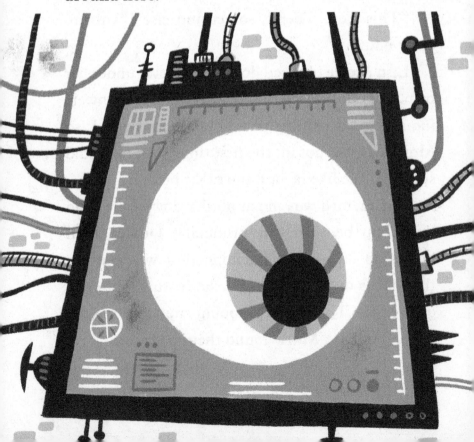

"Mommy Bear?" Vernon snorted. "Why do you call her that?"

"Because she makes sure the machines run *just right*," said Ursine. He saw the blank look on Vernon's face. "You know. Not too hot, not too cold. Just right? Like Mommy Bear's porridge in the story."

Vernon continued to stare blankly. "What story?"

"Goldilocks," Lisa Marie explained. She turned to Ursine. "But it was Baby Bear's porridge that was 'just right.' "

Ursine's thick eyebrows met in a frown. "Was it? Are you sure?"

"Positive," Lisa Marie said.

"Oh," said Ursine. He tapped his foot for a few moments. "Well, probably too late to change it now."

"Probably not worth the bother, no," Lisa Marie agreed. Besides, she was much more interested in something Ursine had said a moment ago. "Mommy Bear is an artificial intelligence?"

"Oh yes. AI is something I've always been

fascinated by." He seemed to swell, becoming more animated. "In fact, that's one of the things about your adventure last night that really excited me. All those bears coming to life, their personalities shaped by the clothes they wore. That was a form of artificial intelligence in itself."

He fished inside his jacket pocket and pulled out a mobile phone. It had been crammed into a case that looked like a large rubber teddy bear's head. Ursine's hairy finger jabbed clumsily at the screen.

"You'll like this. Check it out. I was able to harness the brainwaves of one of the more interesting teddies and re-create it artificially."

Vernon looked from Ursine to Lisa Marie. He clearly had absolutely no idea what was going on and hoped someone was about to explain it all in a slow voice.

Lisa Marie tapped her chin as she thought about all this. "I suppose it makes sense. I mean, the bears didn't have brains, as such, so their intelligence had to be artificial rather than organic."

"I agree," said Vernon, doing his best to look like he was keeping up. "That's just what I was thinking."

"Artificial, and yet this one was fully capable of independent thought!" said Ursine.

"Exactly," Vernon said, nodding. "Yep. I agree."

"Most of them simply followed orders, but this one was something special," Ursine said, holding up his phone. An animated mouth moved on the screen. Combined with the teddy-head phone case, it looked like an actual teddy bear was talking to them.

"Where am I?" a voice growled from the phone's speaker. "What have you done?"

Lisa Marie's blood ran cold. "Oh no. Not him."

"Did those meatbag kids do this to me? I'll rip them apart. I'll tear their arms off!"

"Grizz!" Vernon whispered.

"Turn it off," Lisa Marie urged. "He's dangerous!"

"Yes, I know. Dangerous, but fascinating," Ursine said.

Grizz's voice became an angry hiss. "I hear you, girl! I can hear you. I don't know where you are, but I'll find you. You hear me? I'll find—"

Ursine clicked the sleep button on the phone and the device became silent and dark. "He is an excitable one, isn't he?"

"You have to delete it. Right now," said Lisa Marie.

"Oh, I don't think so. He's much too interesting for that," replied Ursine. "Besides, his entire personality is trapped in here. See?"

He tapped the phone screen and held it up to show Lisa Marie. Nothing happened.

"It's blank," Lisa Marie said.

"Hmm? Oh."

Ursine's pudgy finger tapped the screen again. He waited a moment, then prodded it again. "That's funny."

"What's funny?"

"The software must have crashed or some-thing. It's not responding." Shrugging, he shoved the phone back into his pocket. "Never mind. On with the tour!" He grinned at them through his beard. "You won't believe what I've got next door!"

What Ursine had next door was tanks. A lot of tanks, in fact, all with cannon-like gun turrets on their roofs. They were smaller than Lisa Marie had imagined tanks to be—just the right size for a single teddy bear driver.

And there weren't just tanks. There were miniature jeeps, little motorcyles, and even a squadron of toddler-sized fighter jets. They were assembled in rows in front of a huge roll-up door, ready to move out.

There were two small windows by the door, one on either side. Lisa Marie saw part of a familiar church roof rising into view at the corner of one of them, and realized they must be on the hillside overlooking their town.

But that was impossible. There were no buildings on the hillside. Unless . . .

"It's a bunker," said Ursine, as if reading her mind. "We're in a bunker built into the hill itself. Clever, isn't it?" He stroked his thick beard. "Well, it's more than that, really. It's a whole underground complex. This entire hill is one big building."

Lisa Marie, who had been worrying about the artificial Grizz on Ursine's phone, decided she should probably worry about all this new information for a while instead.

"You're really building an army," she said.

"I am!" Ursine crowed, puffing out his broad chest.

"You do realize this is insane, don't you?"

Ursine's face changed in an instant. For a kidnapper, he'd seemed quite friendly so far, but now his features twisted into a furious scowl as he turned on Lisa Marie.

"Insane? *Insane?* This isn't insanity, it's *genius!*" His big hands grabbed Lisa Marie by the shoulders. His eyes bulged as he roared at her. "I'm not crazy, okay? I'm not crazy!"

"Hey, get your hands off my sister!" said Vernon, but Cuddlyplump and Mr. Fluffton blocked his path before he could step in.

"Do you know how many wars are going on out in the world today? Right now?" Ursine demanded. "Do you know how many crimes are being committed?"

"Like kidnapping?" Vernon asked. Ursine's hench-bears both growled at him.

"My army can stop all that," Ursine continued. "It can bring order to the chaos. I don't want to rule the world, Lisa Marie. Not really. I want to save it, whether it wants to be saved or not."

"What does that mean?" Vernon asked.

Lisa Marie swallowed. "It means he's going to use his bears to take control. They'll force everyone to do everything he says."

"I'm doing it for their own good," Ursine insisted. He released his grip, and his angry scowl was replaced by a smile. "And I want you to help me."

"You what?" said Vernon.

Lisa Marie frowned. "I'll echo that 'You what?' and raise you a 'Huh?'"

"You impressed me, girl. The way you stopped those bears last night. The way you . . ." His

nostrils flared like he'd just smelled a particularly potent fart. ". . . *saved the day*. I'd like you to help me. I'd like you to help me save the world."

Lisa Marie's eyes widened, but before she could reply, she was distracted by several of the delivery-van-sized tubs trundling in through the door. They were all connected like train cars, but nobody appeared to be driving.

Ursine checked his watch. "Aha. Just in time. Kindly observe."

He gestured to where the tubs were rolling to a stop. As they watched, a robotic arm descended from the ceiling. There was a device attached to it that reminded Lisa Marie of the Stuff-U-Lator machine Grizz had used to turn Drake into a teddy bear, only it was much smaller and less homemade looking.

A light shone from the end of it, bathing the

inside of the first tub in a pale blue glow. Lisa Marie held her breath, waiting for something to happen.

Nothing did.

Vernon snorted. "Oh, very impressive," he said, slowly clapping his hands. Mr. Fluffton and Cuddlyplump both snarled at him, showing off some worryingly pointy teeth.

"Look. There!" Lisa Marie whispered.

A paw had emerged from inside the tub. It thudded clumsily against the plastic rim, then flailed around for a moment, as if the person on the other end was trying to figure out how it worked.

A head appeared next, rising into view in a way that was cute and terrifying in roughly equal amounts. The angry-yet-adorable eyes scanned the room, then locked on the group of humans.

"This is a bad idea," Lisa Marie fretted. "You need to stop this."

"Nonsense. They're all under my control," Ursine said.

"That's what Josh thought. The shopkeeper.

Then Grizz told the bears to blast him into microscopic pieces. He thought he could control them, but he couldn't."

Ursine smirked. "Yes. Poor fellow. But it gave me an idea, you see? All these teddies have been fitted with a control chip. Mommy Bear can connect wirelessly and control them remotely. Isn't that right, Mommy?"

"Affirmative," chimed a voice from nowhere in particular. It crackled a little, like the speaker it was playing through was damaged. "Mommy Bear will ensure their behavior is *just right*."

"Are *you* all right, Mommy Bear?" Ursine asked.

There was a lengthy pause before the voice replied. "F-fine. Thank you."

Vernon looked confused. This wasn't a new thing—he had looked confused pretty much from the moment they'd woken up—but he looked more confused now than he had previously.

"So . . . what? They're not really alive? They're robots?"

"No. They're as alive as you or I," said Ursine.

"But the control chips will make sure they don't misbehave."

More heads and paws and the occasional furry bottom had appeared above the rim of the first tub. One or two teddies tumbled out over the edge, while the robotic arm moved on to the second tub and fired up its life-giving light.

As soon as the teddy bears were back on their feet, they snapped to attention, fired off a series of salutes that Lisa Marie couldn't help but find cute and marched over to a door marked WEAPONS AND EQUIPMENT.

"That doesn't bode well," muttered Vernon as they watched the teddies vanish inside.

Ursine spun on his heels to face the children. "Well, Lisa Marie? Have you made a decision?"

Lisa Marie blinked. "About what?"

"About standing by my side, of course! About helping me save the world."

"Why?" Lisa Marie asked.

Ursine frowned. "Why what?"

"Why do you want us to help?"

Ursine hesitated. "Well, I mean . . ." He sighed. "Look, if you must know, being a genius is rather . . . lonely."

Lisa Marie blinked. "Lonely?"

"Yes! It's all very well being super intelligent, but if you don't have anyone of a similar intellect to talk to, it gets so *boring!*"

He puffed up his chest. "Obviously you're nowhere near as smart as I am, but you've got a lot going on between those ears of yours. I've already achieved so much, but with you around to bounce ideas off, there's nothing I couldn't do!"

"So you want us involved because we're smart?" said Vernon.

"*She's* smart," Ursine corrected him, pointing to Lisa Marie. "You're only here because I didn't think she'd agree to be my assistant if I didn't take you too."

Lisa Marie wrinkled her nose. " 'Assistant'?" she said.

"*Senior* assistant!" Ursine said, trying to sweeten the deal. "Executive senior assistant. Think of what we could achieve together!"

Lisa Marie thought of what they could achieve together. She decided she didn't much like it. "No, I don't think I'll bother," she said.

Ursine's face fell. "I'm sorry?"

"I don't think I'll bother," Lisa Marie said. "I think we'll just go home."

"Go . . . *home*?"

"Yes." Lisa Marie nodded. "You said if we weren't interested in your offer, we were free to leave. I'm not interested."

"And neither am I," said Vernon. "Besides, I've got a *Battle War Two* tournament this afternoon, so we need to go."

"No one was asking you," Ursine grunted. He ran his tongue across the front of his teeth and glared down at Lisa Marie. She stared up at him, not blinking or backing down. "Seize them," Ursine commanded.

Cuddlyplump and Mr. Flufftton pounced, grabbing the children around their waists and pinning their arms to their sides. Vernon tried to wriggle free of Mr. Flufftton's grip, but the bear was surprisingly strong for his size.

"Get off. You said you'd let us go!" Lisa Marie yelped.

"Yes. I lied," said Ursine. He winced. "Does that make me a bad person?"

"You're planning to take over the world. You were already a bad person," Lisa Marie pointed out.

"*Save* the world, not take it over," Ursine said, then sniggered. "But yes. Fair point."

He raised his eyes to the ceiling. "Mommy Bear, give me a status update. How are things progressing?"

There was no answer from the speakers.

"Mommy Bear, status update."

Silence followed, broken only by a brief screech of audio feedback.

The lights around the room flickered one at a time, as if someone was testing the switches.

"Huh. That's weird," said Ursine.

"Wait. You said Mommy Bear can connect wirelessly to the teddies," Lisa Marie said. There was an urgency to her voice, like she was trying not to panic. "Right? She connects wirelessly to their chips?"

"Correct," said Ursine. "Why do you ask?"

"Your phone," she said, nodding to Ursine's breast pocket. "Is it connected to the same Wi-Fi network?"

The big man's furry eyebrows knitted themselves together as he frowned. "Yes. Why do you ask?"

Lisa Marie's face turned white. "Turn it off!"

"My phone?"

"Everything! Turn everything off before . . ."

A low chuckle rumbled around the room like thunder.

"Oh no," Lisa Marie whispered. "It's too late. What have you done?"

A voice hissed out of Mommy Bear's speakers. But it wasn't Mommy Bear's voice. It was someone much, *much* worse.

"Well, hey there, meatbags," growled Grizz. "You miss me?"

Ursine tapped his phone, becoming more frantic with every jab.

"I don't understand," he mumbled. "What's going on? Mommy Bear?"

"Mommy Bear isn't home right now," sniggered the voice from the speakers. "I'm in charge now."

"Wait . . . what's happening?" Vernon demanded.

"He made an AI version of Grizz," Lisa Marie explained. She glared at her brother. "The evil monster bear *you* created. And now it's gotten into the computer system."

"And that's bad?" Vernon asked.

"Yes! It's very bad!" Lisa Marie replied.

"Then turn it off," said Vernon. "We should turn it off."

Ursine's mouth flapped open and closed a few times. Lisa Marie felt her heart sink.

"You can't, can you?" she said. "You can't turn it off."

"No," said Ursine. "I never thought I'd need to."

"All this fancy technology and you didn't think to add an off switch?" Vernon spluttered.

"It's fine. It's under control," Ursine insisted. He raised his voice to a shout. "Mommy Bear? Install backup."

Grizz's voice became a menacing growl. "You don't get it, do you, meatbag? There is no Mommy Bear anymore. This whole place is under my control."

Ursine swallowed nervously. "I lied. We're completely doomed."

"Whoa, some of this stuff is cool," Grizz said.

Two robotic arms swung down from the ceiling, their metal pincers snapping at Lisa Marie and Vernon. They yelped and ducked for cover.

"Oh man, I am *so* going to enjoy this," Grizz

laughed. "And let's see. You were saying something about control chips . . . ?"

The door to the Weapons and Equipment room opened and several teddies emerged. They were all dressed in matching military uniforms and carried what looked like toy ray guns in their paws.

There was more movement over at the plastic tubs as dozens of bears clambered out. Although these bears hadn't picked up ray guns, they still had their claws, which was almost as bad.

"Here's what's going to happen," said Grizz. "I'm going to teach you meddling meatbags a lesson you'll remember for the rest of your lives. Luckily for you, that won't be very long."

Vernon looked at his sister. "That almost sounded like a threat."

"Of course it was a threat! He's saying he's going to kill us," Lisa Marie replied.

"That's a bit mean," Vernon whimpered.

"Meh. You did make me a monster," the voice of Grizz pointed out. "And then you got rid of me. So if you ask me, you brought this on yourself."

Two blades unfolded from the robot arms and

began to spin like circular saws. "But I don't want this to be over too quickly, so I'm going to give you a head start."

"That's, uh, very kind of you," said Ursine. "Thanks."

"I meant the kids," Grizz growled. "You, on the other hand, are staying right where you are."

One of the teddy bears opened fire with its ray gun. A beam of red light hit Ursine in his broad chest. He jiggled around, his masses of hair all standing on end as smoke poured from his ears.

"Nnnng!" he grimaced, his teeth rattling together as he toppled backward to the floor like a falling tree.

Cuddlyplump and Mr. Flufton both exchanged worried glances. It took them a moment to figure out what they should do. Both seemed to come to the same conclusion.

"Yeah! Take that, meatbag!" said Cuddlyplump.

"Grizz, Grizz, he's our bear," sang Mr. Flufton, waving his arms around like a cheerleader. "If he can't do it, we don't care!"

Lisa Marie tutted. "Traitors," she said, which brought snarls from both bears.

"Touch her and you'll answer to me!" Grizz snarled. "These meatbags are all mine."

Lisa Marie glared at the bears until they stopped growling.

"How long a head start?" she asked.

"Ten seconds," Grizz said.

"Twenty."

There was a snort from the speakers. "Excuse me?"

"You said you didn't want it to be over too quickly. Ten seconds isn't enough time. Twenty."

"Twelve."

"Fifteen, final offer," said Lisa Marie.

Silence followed. It was eventually broken by a long sigh. "Fine. Fifteen seconds."

"Thank you," said Lisa Marie. "Starting when?"

"Three seconds ago."

"What? That's not fair!" Lisa Marie began, but Vernon caught her by the arm and started dragging her in the direction of the roll-up door.

"Just shut up and run!"

Lisa Marie yanked her arm free. "No. Not that way. It'll be locked. This way."

She banked right and raced back toward the door that led to the main factory floor.

"Are you nuts?" Vernon yelped. "That's not the way out."

"I have an idea. Trust me."

Vernon glanced at the roll-up door, muttered something below his breath, then turned and followed Lisa Marie.

"Five!" announced Grizz, just as they reached the connecting door. "Four."

Sheer terror gave both children an extra burst

of speed. They hurtled through the door just as Grizz bellowed, "Three-two-one!" in one big outburst. Three ray-gun blasts struck the doorframe just as Vernon stumbled safely through.

"After them!" Grizz commanded. His cackle echoed around the entire building. "This is going to be fun."

The enormous digital eye swiveled to look at Lisa Marie and Vernon as they raced onto the factory floor.

"I seeeeeee you," Grizz sang. "You can't escape me, meatbags, and it doesn't look like that teddy pal under your arm is going to save you this time! I'm everywhere!"

As if to prove his point, several more robotic arms sprouted from some of the factory machines. The conveyor belts began to move faster, firing lifeless teddy bears at the children like furry cannonballs.

Lisa Marie ducked a flying bear. Vernon's eyes went wide as he saw the ball of fluff and fur hurtling toward him, but he didn't react in time. It punched him in the face with enough force to send him staggering.

"This way!" Lisa Marie urged. She grabbed Vernon by the arm and they raced toward the last machine, dodging a barrage of flying stuffed toys. Behind them, the doorway was suddenly filled with ray-gun-toting teddies.

"What now?" Vernon yelped as he and Lisa Marie reached the machine.

Lisa Marie pulled her brother around to the other side of the machine and up onto the conveyor belt. Vernon babbled in terror as they were both whisked inside the machine.

"We can't hide in here!"

"We're not hiding," said Lisa Marie. The conveyor belt jerked to a stop. A light on top of the machine flashed red. "We're being rejected."

A hatch opened beneath them. The children caught a brief glimpse of a long metal chute. Then gravity grabbed them and they fell, screaming, into the dark.

Lisa Marie quickly crossed her ankles, tucked Bearvis tighter under her arm, and straightened her back. She slid smoothly down the chute like a luge rider at the Winter Olympics. Just above her, Vernon thumped and thudded off the sides, leaving dents wherever he hit the metal.

"Ow! Oof! That hurt!"

With a *whoosh*, Lisa Marie slid out of the chute, hit a net at the bottom, then flopped down onto a pile of soft teddy bears.

A moment later, Vernon was fired out like a missile. He wailed as he overshot the net, then hit the wall behind it with a *crunch*. He hung there for a moment, arms and legs spread in an X shape, before sliding slowly to the floor.

Lisa Marie rolled down from the mound of teddies, gave Bearvis a quick check to make sure he was okay, then helped Vernon up.

"What were you thinking?" he yelped. "You could have killed us!"

"Grizz *definitely* would have killed us," Lisa Marie pointed out. "This seemed like a sensible solution."

"Sensible? I just got fired at a wall!" Vernon reminded her. He was silenced by Lisa Marie's hand clamping across his mouth.

"Shhh!" she whispered. "Not so loud."

The room they had landed in was mostly dark, with just a faint glow spilling through a gap at the bottom of a door. They could hear liquid burbling through pipes, and the occasional *drip-drip-drip* of a leak.

Lisa Marie waited for her eyes to adjust to the darkness. They were in a spooky old basement. Still, at least there weren't any eyes watching them from screens, and so far, Grizz's voice hadn't crackled from any hidden speakers.

There was a sudden glow as Vernon checked his phone.

"Still no signal," he whispered.

"That's hardly surprising. We're in the basement of an underground complex built into a hill," Lisa Marie pointed out.

"I can't get on the Wi-Fi, either," Vernon moaned. "It's password protected."

He sighed and slipped his phone back into his pocket. "Great. Drake's going to be furious if I'm not online for the tournament."

Lisa Marie tutted. "I think that's the least of our problems."

Vernon pointed to the mouth of the chute they'd emerged from. A terrible thought had just occurred to him. "What if they follow us?" he whispered.

Lisa Marie shook her head. "Ursine said it opens for the duds that don't pass quality control. The other bears all passed the checks, so they can't get in."

She was about to add "We should be safe for now," when she heard the soft scuff of footsteps and saw a shadow moving in the light from under the door.

"I don't think we're alone," she said, making her voice as soft as possible. She pointed to the door. "There's someone through there."

Vernon gulped. "Do you think it's someone nice?"

There was the *thunk* of a lock sliding open on the other side of the door.

"Looks like we're about to find out," Lisa Marie whispered.

To Lisa Marie's surprise, Vernon stepped protectively in front of her, his fists raised. "If I say 'run,' then you run," he instructed. "I'll catch up."

The door opened, flooding the basement with light. Roaring, Vernon charged at the figure who appeared in the doorway, flailing his arms around like a windmill.

WHUMP!

The door slammed closed in his face. Vernon stumbled back, clutching his forehead. He crashed into Lisa Marie, knocking them both on to the floor.

Lisa Marie sighed. "My hero."

The door creaked open once more, and a teddy bear's head peeked out. Its fur was mostly gray, and it wore a pair of half-moon glasses on the end of its nose.

"Hello?" the bear said in a soft, croaky voice. "Who's there?"

"Um, hi. I'm Lisa Marie. This is my brother, Vernon," said Lisa Marie, standing up and dusting herself off.

Now that she was back on her feet, she realized this teddy bear was much smaller than the ones upstairs. He was around the same size as Bearvis, but looked shorter thanks to a stoop in his back.

"Please, don't hurt us!" Vernon whimpered.

"Hurt you? Oh my! Oh no! No, I wouldn't dream of it!"

The teddy tilted his head back so he could peer at them through his spectacles. "Oh my, you *have* been put together wrong, haven't you? You poor things. I mean, just look at your faces," he said, shuddering in horror.

Lisa Marie and Vernon both frowned. "What's wrong with our faces?" asked Lisa Marie.

"Yeah. You're not exactly going to win any beauty contests yourself, dude," added Vernon.

"You've got no fur, for starters. And your eyes are all wrong," the old bear said. "And you're too big, *far* too big. I mean, your heads are all like . . ." He puffed out his cheeks as far as they'd go. "Like that."

Lisa Marie shook her head. "We're not teddy bears."

"You aren't?" the old bear gasped. "Are you sure?"

"We're sure," said Lisa Marie. "We're human."

"Are you? Well, I never. Well, I never. I mean . . .

I suppose that would explain a lot. Sorry, it's just that it's generally, only bears that come down the chute. I'm not used to anyone else dropping in."

He held a paw out to them. "Theodore Steiffenhume the Third," he said grandly. He started to bow, but his back made a twanging noise, so he stopped. "A pleasure to make your acquaintance."

Vernon's eyes narrowed. "Hold on . . . you're not planning a sneak attack, are you?"

"Heavens, no. Why on earth would I want to do that?" asked Theodore Steiffenhume III. "Besides your bizarre and frankly monstrous appearance, I mean."

"The other bears we've met . . . ," began Lisa Marie. She looked down at Bearvis. "Well, most of them—they're all evil. They want to take over the world."

"I say!" said Theodore. He shook his head. "Goodness, no. Nothing like that going on down here. It's just me and the duds, minding our own business."

Lisa Marie looked back at the little pile of teddies she had landed on. "Are those the duds?"

"Some of them. The ones I haven't gotten to yet," said Theodore. He peered at the children over the top of his glasses. "Would you like to see the others?"

Lisa Marie chewed her lip. "I don't know. Can Mommy Bear see what we're doing down here?"

"She cannot," Theodore said. "She brought me to life so that I might keep things shipshape down here. It was all getting rather clogged up before I was sent in to sort it all out."

"How long have you been here?" Lisa Marie asked.

Theodore shrugged his stooped shoulders. "Oh, I don't know. A while. The fellow running the place—Him Upstairs, I call him—doesn't like to be reminded of his failures, apparently, so I'm left to my own devices. I'm not even certain he knows I exist." The elderly teddy shook his head sadly. "The basement area is completely cut off from Mommy Bear. It's a shame, really. She knows some terribly funny jokes."

"Not anymore," Vernon muttered.

"I'm sorry?"

"Nothing."

Theodore blinked a few times, then nod-ded. "Right. Well . . ." He gestured to the open door behind him and smiled an imperfect smile. "Shall we?"

9

Vernon leaned in close to Lisa Marie's ear and whispered so Theodore Steiffenhume III didn't hear him.

"Well, this place is horrible."

Lisa Marie couldn't really argue. Theodore had led them into a large room that was lit all around with old-fashioned oil lamps. Rusty pipes ran along the exposed brick walls. Damp patches bloomed on the ceiling, and there were even little clumps of mushrooms growing in some of the corners. Lisa Marie immediately recognized them from the *Bumper Book of Poisonous Things* she'd once borrowed from the library and made a mental note not to get too close.

None of these things were the most disturbing part of the room, though. That honor went to the teddy bears.

There were a hundred or more of them, all different shapes and sizes. They hung from the pipes on lengths of rope that were wrapped around their tummies, their arms dangling limply, their glassy eyes staring at the floor below.

That didn't apply to all of them, though, Lisa Marie realized. Some of them didn't have paws. Or eyes. Or even tummies, in some cases. At least half of them looked unfinished, like they'd been stitched together wrong, and several were oozing stuffing out of holes in their seams.

There were one-legged teddies, no-legged teddies and at least a couple with three legs. One had had its face put on upside down, while another's huge ears sprouted from the side of its head like the handles of a trophy.

If you ignored their missing parts, most of the bears were the same size as those being made in the factory, but a couple were Bearvis-sized, and one was so small Lisa Marie could've held it in the palm of her hand with room to spare.

"Look at that one," Vernon whispered, pointing to another. "It's just a head on a foot."

"Yes, terrible shame!" Theodore called back over his shoulder. "Poor fellow. I call him Sir Hopsalot."

He began to gesture around the room. "That's Jimmy Three Legs. Uncle Noface. Tiny Norman."

"You named them all?" said Lisa Marie.

"Of course! Why wouldn't I?"

"Uh, because it's creepy and weird?" Vernon said.

Lisa Marie elbowed him in the ribs. "Ignore him. I name all my teddy bears."

"Which proves my point," Vernon said.

Lisa Marie spotted something half hidden by a sheet in the corner. It was big and bulky, with a tangle of wires coiled up at the bottom. There was something familiar about the shape.

"What's that?"

Theodore followed her gaze, then let out a little yelp. "Oh, nothing, nothing. Don't worry about that. Nothing to see there."

He was too late. Lisa Marie crossed to the sheet and pulled it away. Her eyes widened when she saw what had been hidden beneath it.

"It's one of Ursine's machines. This brings bears to life, doesn't it?"

"What? No! That thing? No!" Theodore said, wringing his paws together. He sighed. "I mean . . . yes. It should. Don't tell anyone, but I stole it from the garbage. Him Upstairs was throwing it away, and I just thought . . . Well, it would be nice to have some company."

"Why didn't you use it?" Vernon wondered.

"It's broken. I tried to fix it, but . . ." He tapped his head. "It's all just stuffing up here, you see? I'm built for cuddling, not electrical engineering. I probably should have thrown it away, but it was hard enough to drag down here without anyone seeing me, so I just left it." The old bear suddenly looked very nervous. "You won't tell on me, will you? I could get into terrible trouble."

Lisa Marie blew some dust off the machine's control panel and tugged gently on some loose wiring.

"I promise we won't tell anyone," she said. "*If you do me a favor.*"

"A favor? What kind of favor?" Theodore asked.

Lisa Marie grinned. "Find me a screwdriver."

"What do you want a screwdriver for?" Vernon asked.

Lisa Marie glanced down at Bearvis. "We're bringing back the King."

A teddy bear in a frilly pink tutu halted in front of the giant-eye screen and snapped a salute. The eye glared down at the bear for a few long silent moments.

"What *are* you wearing?" Grizz's voice eventually demanded.

"It's a tutu, sir!" barked the bear, performing another crisp salute.

Grizz sighed. "I can see it's a tutu. I suppose what I really want to know is *why* are you wearing it?"

"We ran out of army uniforms, sir!" the bear replied, saluting again. "But we found some other outfits in one of the storerooms, so we're wearing them."

Grizz's voice became a menacing growl. "So

let me get this straight. Half of my terrifying teddy bear army is dressed as ballerinas?"

"Oh, no, sir," said the bear, firing off yet another salute. "There were only a few tutus. The rest was a mix of other stuff. We've got some Vikings, a few pirates . . ."

"That sounds more promising," said Grizz.

"Lollipop ladies, clowns, funny little penguins . . ."

Grizz sighed again. "Those are less promising. But *enough*. Give me a progress report."

"Ursine Kodiak has been restrained as requested, sir!" the soldier-bear replied.

"And those little meatbag kids . . . ?"

"Um, we're still searching, sir! Cuddlyplump and Mr. Fluffton are making their way to the basement. We think the children are—"

"You *think*?" Grizz's voice barked, making the speakers rattle and buzz. On-screen, the eye blazed furiously. "I don't want *think*, I want them *found*."

"Sir, yes, sir!" the soldier-bear said, stiffening and saluting again. He performed a crisp about-face.

"Wait," said Grizz.

The soldier-bear did another about-face so he was facing the screen.

"On second thought, don't bother. They'll come to us soon enough. Everyone get ready."

"Uh, ready for what, sir?"

"Ready to get in those tanks and planes, of course." Grizz's voice became an excited rumble. "We're going to take over the world!"

"Sir, yes, sir!"

The soldier-bear turned again.

"Hang on. I wasn't finished."

The soldier-bear turned yet again. If this kept up, he was going to get dizzy.

"The big meatbag. The grown-up. What did you call him again?"

"Ursine Kodiak, sir!"

"Have him brought here."

A robotic arm reached into a container fixed to the side of one of the machines and pulled out a tiny microchip no bigger than a postage stamp.

"I've just had a truly diabolical idea!"

"Very good, sir!" replied the bear. Then, with a curtsy, he rose on to the tips of his furry feet, raised his hands gracefully above his head and danced his way to the exit.

Lisa Marie's head and shoulders were fully inside the machine. Her voice echoed as she called out to Vernon.

"Okay, I think I have it this time. The thermocouple had a loose capacitor."

"That's the *first* thing I'd have checked," Vernon lied. "The thermo . . . thingy."

"Should we switch it on?" asked Theodore.

"Only if you want to chop my head off," Lisa Marie replied.

Vernon's finger hovered above the power button. "Tempting . . ."

Lisa Marie quickly pulled her top half out of the machine and glared up at her brother. He flashed her a grin. "I wouldn't actually have pressed it," he said. "You know, unless you got *really* annoying."

There was a bit on the front of the machine that looked like an old car headlight. It creaked as Lisa Marie angled it at a spot on the floor.

"You sure about this?" Vernon asked.

Lisa Marie took a deep breath, then nodded. "It's going to work. It has to. I've checked all the components, and everything seems to be in place."

"You don't want to test it first?"

"There might not be time," Lisa Marie said. She closed her eyes for a moment, whispered something hopeful-sounding, then positioned Bearvis so the headlight was pointing straight at him.

"Vernon, Theodore Steiffenhume the Third, you might want to stand back," she warned them. "Just in case anything does go wrong."

"Very good," said Theodore, retreating a few steps. Vernon stood his ground beside her.

"I trust you," he said, offering her a reassuring smile.

"Thanks," Lisa Marie said. She placed her finger lightly on the power button. "Here goes."

She pushed the button.

There was a *hummmmmmmmmm*.

There was a flash.

There was a *bang*.

Bearvis bounced off the floor, thudded against the ceiling and ricocheted off at a steep angle. He rocketed across the room, then crashed into a stack of cardboard boxes, spilling glassy eyes and plastic noses all over the floor.

The boxes collapsed, burying the motionless teddy bear.

Vernon took a single sidestep away from Lisa Marie and the machine. "Yep," he said. "Totally should've tested it."

"Oh no! Bearvis!" Lisa Marie cried. She had just started to run to him when a door was thrown open at the far end of the room.

"Get off!"

"You get off!"

Cuddlyplump and Mr. Fluffton tumbled in, slapping at each other. It was only when they spotted Lisa Marie and the others that they stopped.

"Well, well, well," growled Cuddlyplump.

"What do we have here?" snarled Mr. Fluffton.

"It's them kids," said Cuddlyplump.

Mr. Fluffton tutted. "Yes, I know. I was being . . . what do you call it?"

"An idiot?" Cuddlyplump guessed.

"No. Menacing. I was being menacing."

"Oh. Right. Gotcha."

Both bears advanced, their hard plastic claws extending from inside their paws.

"If you go down in the chute today, you're sure of a big surprise . . . ," Mr. Fluffton sang, a wicked grin creeping across his face. "If you go down in the chute today, you're probably going to cry. . . ."

Lisa Marie stood up straight. "You're not scaring us."

"They are a bit," Vernon mumbled.

Theodore blocked the other bears' path. "Now, now, enough of that," he warned. "I won't put up with any bullying behavior down here."

Cuddlyplump bared his teeth and pounced,

knocking Theodore over and pinning him to the floor. "Oh yeah, old man?" he demanded. "And what are you going to do about it?"

"Leave him alone!" Lisa Marie cried. "Get off him, you bully."

Mr. Flufton snarled at her. "Don't worry about him. Worry about—"

A heavy cardboard box landed on him, flattening him against the floor. Groaning, he tried to push the box away, but something landed on top of it with a *thud,* pinning him down.

Lisa Marie's eyes widened. There, crouching on the box in a karate pose, was a black-pompadoured teddy in a sparkling sequined suit.

"Pardon me, son," drawled the newcomer in a deep Southern accent. "But that ain't no way to talk to a young lady."

"Bearvis!" cried Lisa Marie. "You're alive!"

"You bet your boots I am, little darlin'," Bearvis said. He winked at her. "Now, excuse me while I take care of business."

With a twitch of his legs, Bearvis backflipped dramatically off the top of the box. He spun in the air, his cape billowing around him like a superhero's.

Then he misjudged the landing and thumped, face-first, to the floor.

"My fault. No harm done," he muttered. "Totally got this under control."

Picking himself up, he smoothed back his hair. "Now, where was I?" he asked, just as the much larger Cuddlyplump slammed into him, sending both bears tumbling and rolling across the room in a blur of fur and sequins.

"So that's how it's gonna be, huh? Hit a guy when he ain't ready?" said Bearvis. "That's low, man. That's real low."

Cuddlyplump's face twisted into a snarl. "I don't know who you are, but you made a big mistake messing with us."

"Son, the only one who has made a mistake here is you," Bearvis told him. "Also, on a side note, your breath stinks like a skunk's behind. You might want to try mouthwash."

Cuddlyplump lunged with his claws, but Bearvis neatly sidestepped out of his path. Twisting, he delivered a spinning roundhouse kick to the back of the bigger bear's legs. Cuddlyplump grunted as he tripped, fell and smacked his head on another of the boxes.

"Very nicely done, my boy!" cheered Theodore, dragging himself to his feet.

"Thank you. Thank you very much," drawled Bearvis.

Lisa Marie and Vernon quickly pulled two of the lifeless bears down from where they were dangling and unhooked their ropes. With Bearvis's help, they tied Ursine's hench-bears together, being sure to bind their arms in a way that meant they couldn't use their claws to cut themselves free.

That done, Lisa Marie grabbed Bearvis and pulled him into a teddy-sized bear hug. "You're back!" she cheered. "I knew you'd come back!"

"Of course I am, honey. And it sure is good to see you too."

Vernon sighed. "Touching as all this is," he said, staring down at the two tightly bound teddy villains, "if these two idiots found us, then the rest won't be far behind. I really hope you've got a plan."

Lisa Marie smiled up at her brother. "I'm working on it. But first . . ." She crossed her arms and turned to the captive hench-bears. "We're going to need some information."

Ursine Kodiak was having a pretty nasty dream about being chased by bees. He was running for his life on his undersized feet, but running wasn't really his strong point, so he wasn't going very fast.

One bee in particular was determined to sting him on the head. He kept thrashing his walking stick out at it, trying to chase it away. Deep down, though, he knew the bee was going to catch him. He knew it was just a matter of time before—

Ow!

The bee's stinger stabbed him just behind his right ear. The sharp pain of the sting was enough to wake Ursine up.

"Yeowch!" he yelped, slapping a hand to the side of his head. He could still feel where the bee had stung him, even though he now knew there hadn't actually been any bees at all.

Ursine felt a tingling at the back of his neck. It was no more than a tickle, really, but it made him feel like he was being watched. Like some secret observer was spying on him, watching his every move.

"Ahem."

Ursine looked up to find an enormous digital eye glaring down at him from a few meters away.

"Wakey-wakey, meatbag," Grizz's voice spat. "Had a good sleep?"

"Not particularly," said Ursine. He found his cane on the floor beside him and started the awkward process of getting to his feet. "Now, I don't know exactly what's going on, but I'm putting a stop to it right—"

"Sit down," Grizz commanded.

Ursine sat down.

This confused him. He hadn't planned to sit down. He'd actively been against the idea of sitting down, in fact. And yet, here he was. Sitting down.

He tugged sharply on his beard. Again, this was not something he had planned to do. His arm had raised on its own, before giving the hair on his chin a short, sharp yank.

"Um," he said, then he shoved two fingers up his nose as far as they'd go and wriggled them around. It was really quite unpleasant, but somehow he couldn't stop it.

The other hand came up unexpectedly, flicked his left ear, went *wibblewibblewibble* with his bottom lip, then started slapping him across both cheeks, one after the other.

"Stop hitting yourself. Stop hitting yourself. Stop hitting yourself," sniggered Grizz.

"What is this?" Ursine demanded between slaps. "What's going on?"

"It's justice, that's what," said Grizz. "A meat-bag puts control chips in teddy bears' heads, and you think I'm going to just let that pass? Nuh-uh. No way. Not on my watch. You know the phrase 'What's good for the goose is good for the gander'? Well, swap in 'teddy bear' for 'goose' and 'disgusting human meatbag' for 'gander.'"

Ursine blinked several times. "Huh? You've lost me."

"No, okay, that came out more complicated

than it was supposed to. It sounded better in my head. Or digital eye. Or whatever I have now," Grizz admitted. "The point is, those control chips you were sticking in the heads of my brothers and sisters? I stuck one in yours."

Ursine gasped. "You didn't!" he whimpered, then jabbed himself in both eyes, squeezed the end of his nose, and pulled sharply on his tongue, all without meaning to.

"Oh, I totally did," said Grizz. "And if you want me to take it out, you're going to use that big brain of yours to help me."

"H-how?"

Though he had no mouth, the smile could be heard in Grizz's voice. "You're going to build me a body."

Cuddlyplump and Mr. Flufton both stared in horror as Vernon approached them, an electric razor buzzing in his hand. Lisa Marie, Bearvis and Theodore were gathered behind him, watching.

"You wouldn't!" Mr. Flufton whimpered.

"He would," said Lisa Marie.

"She's right. I totally would," Vernon agreed. He flicked a button on the side of the razor, cranking up the speed. The low buzz became a high-pitched whine.

Theodore turned away. "Oh, I can't look!"

"The boy's gonna shave y'all bald," Bearvis told the hench-bears. "I suggest y'all start talking, lickety-split."

"Never!" yelped Cuddlyplump. "We'll never talk in a million—"

Vernon brought the razor closer.

"Okay, okay, we'll talk!" Cuddlyplump wailed. "Just don't shave us!"

Vernon stepped back and cranked the razor down to a slow hum. Lisa Marie and Bearvis took his spot, their arms folded as they began their interrogation.

"What's Grizz planning?" Lisa Marie demanded.

Bearvis's eyes widened. "Grizz? That crazy monster-dude? I thought he was done for."

"He's back. Sort of," Lisa Marie said. "It's a long story."

"Oh man. That's all kindsa bad news," Bearvis mumbled. He jabbed a paw at the two henchbears. "Y'all better start talking. The King don't like to be kept waiting."

"We don't know anything!" Mr. Fluffton protested. "All we know is he took over Mommy Bear, and now he controls everything. The teddies, the tanks, the jets."

Bearvis's eyes grew even wider. "Wait a minute, wait a minute. Tanks and jets? I kinda feel like I'm missing a lot of details here."

"Grizz has an army," Vernon said. "There. Now you're all caught up."

"He sent us down to find you," Cuddlyplump said. "We were supposed to bring you back. That's all we know."

"So he doesn't know exactly where we are?" Lisa Marie asked.

Both hench-bears shook their heads. "No. He just knows you're in the basement. There's no security down here. Mommy Bear can't see anything on this level."

"We know. Which means neither can Grizz," said Lisa Marie. "Okay, that's good. That should mean we have time to come up with a plan."

Vernon raised his hand. "I've got one. It starts with 'run' and ends with 'away.'"

"That was my original plan," said Lisa Marie. "But we can't run. We need to find out what Grizz is up to. We have to stop him."

"That's what the police are for!" said Vernon.

"You think the police are going to believe us if we tell them an evil artificial intelligence is controlling an army of teddy bears?" Lisa Marie asked.

"We've got proof!" Vernon pointed out. "We can show them Bearvis."

"We can't do that!" Lisa Marie gasped. "They'd take him to a lab or something."

"So? What's the worst that could happen?"

"They might dissect him."

Vernon hesitated. "Okay, yeah, that *is* pretty bad."

Bearvis shook his head. "Ain't no one cutting up the King."

"Is it safe to look yet?" asked Theodore, peeking back over his shoulder. When he saw that nobody was about to be shaved, he turned around.

"If I may be so bold," he continued. "If these two hooligans aren't going to prove helpful, it seems the only alternative is to go and take a peek at what's going on up there for yourselves."

Lisa Marie and Bearvis exchanged glances, then nodded. Vernon groaned. "Ugh. I guess."

"There are two ways that you might observe the goings-on up there," Theodore explained. "The easy way, and the hard way. Which would you prefer?"

"The easy way," Vernon said, jumping in quickly before anyone could suggest otherwise. "Definitely the easy way."

"Very good," said Theodore. Then he frowned. "Wait. Hold on."

He rubbed his chin, deep in thought. "No. Sorry. I was thinking about something else. There's only the hard way, I'm afraid." He clapped his paws together and smiled encouragingly. "Still, I'm sure you'll be up to the challenge."

A flicker of doubt crossed his furry face.

"Well, I'm not *sure,* exactly. But I'm confident."

He looked them up and down.

"Ish."

12

Lisa Marie squeaked up the air duct, her elbows and knees jammed against the walls as she shimmied herself along. Bearvis was below her, with Vernon following. Vernon was indulging in one of his favorite hobbies—complaining.

"Can you please get your butt out of my face?" he grumbled.

"How about you get your face outta my butt?" Bearvis replied.

"Shhh!" Lisa Marie urged. "Someone might hear us."

They had been climbing for three or four minutes now. At first the narrow tunnel had led up gradually at a shallow angle, but now they were climbing straight upward. One slip, Lisa Marie knew, and they'd all go tumbling down.

"I can't believe this is how I'm spending my Saturday," Vernon mumbled. "Stuck in a tube with a teddy's butt in my face. I should be at home playing Xbox."

"Saving the real world is a *little* more important than saving some fantasy-game world," Lisa Marie pointed out.

"You try telling Drake that," Vernon said. "If I miss the tournament, he's going to kill me!"

Lisa Marie's voice became a scratchy whisper. "Stop. We're here."

She stopped climbing at a slatted metal grate and wedged her back against the wall directly across from it so she could see through the gaps.

"What's happening?" asked Vernon. "What can you see?"

Lisa Marie couldn't see very much. The gaps in the grate were narrow, and she couldn't get close enough to look through them without risking a nasty fall.

"Not a lot," she admitted.

While she couldn't see much, she could hear plenty. There were a lot of soft footsteps all marching in time, the *clack* of ray guns being loaded and the low growling of engines firing up. It sounded like the army was getting organized for something big.

"Hold on. Let me check it out, honey," Bearvis whispered. He clambered up Lisa Marie, almost choking her when his paw slipped into her mouth. "Pardon me. My fault."

He perched himself on Lisa Marie's legs, which were wedged against the same wall the metal grate was on. Shuffling forward, he brought his face up close to the gaps and peered out.

"Can you see anything?" Lisa Marie whispered.

"I can see all kinds of things," said Bearvis. "Ain't one of them good. You were right, they got an army. Big, too. Looks like they're loading up to move on out."

The sound of Vernon gulping echoed tinnily inside the air duct. "How many?"

"Uh, gimme a sec," said Bearvis. He began to count below his breath. "One, two, three, four, five, six . . ." He tutted. "Aw man, they keep moving. Hold on, I got this. One, two, three—"

"Just roughly will do," said Lisa Marie.

"Oh. Okay. In that case, if I had to guess—you know, estimate, or whatever? I'd say . . . a lot."

Vernon sighed. "A lot?"

"A whole lot. A whole *bunch*, in fact."

"Well, that was helpful," Vernon said. "Thanks."

"Y'all don't mention it," Bearvis said.

There was a sudden *screech* of bending metal and the grate was torn away by a robotic arm, flooding the duct with light. "Well, well, well," boomed Grizz's voice. It came from all around them at once. "Found you!"

With the grate gone, Lisa Marie caught a glimpse of the fully assembled army. "A whole bunch" had been an understatement. There were hundreds of bears out there now. Thousands, maybe. Most of them looked ready for war, although a surprising number looked ready for piracy, ballet and helping children cross busy roads.

A squadron of colorfully dressed clowns broke ranks and began cartwheeling toward the open vent. Lisa Marie swallowed. There was only one thing for it.

"Vernon, brace yourself!"

"Oh, not again!" Vernon yelped. Then his sister slammed into him and they both slid clumsily down the duct, *thonk*ing and *thud*ding off the sides, with Bearvis tumbling along behind.

Vernon hit the slope first. He slid down it headfirst, one arm stretched out ahead of him, the other pinned by his side. He shut his eyes and braced himself for impact, then felt a sudden sensation

of weightlessness as he flew out of the vent and across the room.

Lisa Marie tumbled out next, followed by Bearvis. They both, to Vernon's dismay, landed on top of him.

Theodore shuffled across and peered over his glasses at the tangle of arms, legs and paws.

"Well?" he asked. "How did it go?"

"Grate!"

Theodore smiled. "Really? Oh, that *is* good news!"

"No, not *great*, I mean the *grate*! Shut the

grate!" Lisa Marie yelped, untangling herself. She rushed over to the air vent and heaved the metal grate into place just as the first of the clown bears slammed against it from the other side, making its bright red nose honk. Another clown and two soldiers appeared behind it and began forcing the grate off the vent.

"Vernon, help!" Lisa Marie cried, jamming the metal barrier with her hip to stop the bears from pushing through.

Vernon stumbled upright and ran over to join her. He added his weight to hers as the bears shoved harder, hatred blazing in their glassy eyes.

"Ha! Now you're in for it!" snorted Mr. Fluffton.

"Yeah, ain't so tough now, are you?" sneered Cuddlyplump.

"Shut up or we'll shave you!" Lisa Marie warned them.

"What do we do?" Vernon asked. "We can't hold them forever."

"It's only three or four teddy bears," Bearvis pointed out.

A series of *thud*s followed as half a dozen more bears slid down the ramp. "Or, you know, ten to fifteen," Bearvis continued. He swished his paws around and kicked the air. "Nothing the King can't handle. I say let them come at me."

"Are you nuts?" Vernon cried. "It's not just ten to fifteen. There's a whole army up there."

Lisa Marie stiffened. "A whole army."

"That's what I just said!" Vernon scowled.

"A whole army!"

"We know! You don't have to keep saying it!"

Lisa Marie shook her head. "No, you don't understand. I don't mean them. I mean us."

Vernon, who spent much of his time looking confused, really outdid himself this time. "Huh?"

"No time to explain!" Lisa Marie said. She pressed her back against the air-vent grate and braced her feet on the floor. She beckoned to Bearvis. "Come and help Vernon hold this," she instructed.

"Ten-four, little darlin.' "

She waited until Bearvis had squeezed in between her and her brother before stepping away.

"Good. Now, Theodore, round up the Duds while I fire up the machine."

Theodore glanced around at all the lifeless bears dangling from ropes around the room. "The Duds? Why, whatever for?"

A look of determination swept across Lisa Marie's face. "We're building ourselves an army!"

13

It wasn't fair.

Ursine Kodiak had spent years studying science and dark magic so that he could one day build a device that would bring teddy bears to life. It had taken two decades and a small fortune, but he'd finally achieved his lifelong ambition. He didn't really like to blow his own trumpet, but he was *definitely* the greatest genius who had ever lived.

And now what? He was being pushed around by his own creation, forced to punch himself in the face or slap himself on the bottom whenever he didn't work fast enough.

"Ow! Will you cut that out?" he complained, after a particularly devastating right hook that almost knocked him to the floor. "That hurts, you know!"

"Of course I know, meatbag. Why else would I be making you hit yourself? You think I'm doing it for fun?" Grizz's voice demanded. He sniggered. "Actually, I'm totally doing it for fun. This is hilarious."

To prove his point, Grizz made Ursine grab the back of his own underpants and pull them up into a painful wedgie.

"Stop it! I've got three PhDs! I'm part he-witch! You can't just use me like a puppet."

"Oh, I can and I will," said Grizz. "Now, attach that pointy thing to the round part. And don't forget the chain saws. I want chain saws. And a laser. Do we have a laser?"

Ursine shook his head. "No. No laser." He tweaked his nose, then poked himself in the eye. "Ow!"

"Then find me a laser!" Grizz demanded. His voice came as an evil, sinister hiss. "I want this to be *perfect*."

Down in the basement, things were not going well. Lisa Marie had tried the machine on five different Duds, but none of them had so much as twitched, let alone come to life.

Meanwhile, the air duct was becoming crammed with angry teddies and Vernon and

Bearvis were now struggling to hold the grate in place.

Lisa Marie fiddled with the control panel. "Maybe I need to recalibrate the focusing beam . . . ," she said.

"There's no time!" Vernon yelped. "Do something else!"

"Like what?"

"How should I know? You're the smart one!"

Lisa Marie was a modest sort of girl and felt like she should probably argue. The fact of the matter, though, was that Vernon was right. She wasn't good at very many things, but she was clever, and clever was what they needed right now.

She pointed to the machine. "Theodore, recalibrate the focus beam!"

Theodore stared blankly back at her. "I have no idea what those words mean."

"Flip those switches, then try again," Lisa Marie explained, then turned to where Vernon and Bearvis were struggling with the grate.

"Think, Lisa Marie, think," she whispered.

She closed her eyes and tried to block out the growling and snarling of the bears on the other side of the grate. There had to be a solution. There had to be.

She thought back over everything that had happened so far. The black car. Ursine Kodiak. The artificial intelligence version of Grizz.

No, none of those was the answer.

The army. Jets. Tanks.

No, that wasn't it.

The Duds. The hench-bears. The control chips.

Lisa Marie's eyes flicked open. *The control chips.*

"Vernon, give me your phone!" she barked.

Jamming his back against the grate, Vernon fished in his pocket. "There's no signal."

"There's no *phone* signal," Lisa Marie said. She let out a yelp of excitement when she checked the display. "But there *is* a Wi-Fi signal!"

"But we don't know the password!" Vernon pointed out.

Spinning on her heels, Lisa raced over to Cuddlyplump and Mr. Fluffton. "These two do. What's the Wi-Fi password?"

"Pah! We'll never tell you," sneered Mr. Fluffton.

"Theodore, bring me the razor!" Lisa Marie ordered.

"Okay, Okay, we'll talk!" sobbed Cuddlyplump. "It's *Ursine is a genius,* all lowercase and all one word."

Lisa Marie began frantically tapping on the screen.

"You might wanna get a move on, honey," Bearvis urged, gritting his teeth as he pushed back on the grate. "Getting hard to hold 'em all back."

"But the *E* in *genius* is a number three," Cuddlyplump added.

Lisa Marie tutted, deleted a few letters, then finished typing the rest of the code. "Come on, come on," she whispered, watching a little timer on the screen spin around. "Yes! I'm in!"

"Great!" Vernon cheered. "Um, now what?"

Lisa Marie stared down at the phone screen.

"I think the control chips are a weak spot. I just need to figure out how to connect to them. . . ."

"Then do it quick!" Vernon groaned, his face turning red with the effort of holding the bears back. "Because they're coming through!"

He was sent stumbling across the room as the weight of the teddies became too much. The grate fell outward, pinning Bearvis beneath it as a squadron of soldiers, clowns, pirates and one bear dressed as a tiny elephant thundered into the room.

14

"Hey! Watch it! Ow!" Bearvis groaned as the invading bears trampled over him.

The teddies fanned out in a semicircle, their glassy eyes fixed on Lisa Marie, their mouths twisted into angry snarls. The soldier-bears raised their ray guns. The pirates waggled their cutlasses. The clown bears produced custard pies from inside their oversized striped pants and took aim. The bear dressed as an elephant waggled his trunk and wondered if he should've chosen a different costume.

Lisa Marie frantically tapped on the phone screen as the bears all prepared to pounce. For a moment, it looked like she was done for—but then a misshapen figure *boing*ed to a stop in front of her, blocking the advancing teddies' path.

"Back off, chaps! Unless you'd care to answer to Sir Hopsalot!"

Lisa Marie glanced over to where Theodore had been operating the machine, then joined everyone else in staring at the new arrival. A few of the baddie bears sniggered as they peered down at Sir Hopsalot teetering unsteadily in front of them on his single paw.

"I advise you not to laugh, gentlemen," Sir Hopsalot warned. "Or I'll be forced to slap some manners into you."

"Arrr! With what?" snorted one of the pirate bears. "You ain't got no arms."

"You's just a head on a foot," added one of the soldier-bears.

The elephant bear trumpeted in agreement.

Sir Hopsalot's eyes darted left and right, searching for shoulders that weren't there.

"Oh. Well. That is a problem," he admitted. He shrugged, which was impressive, given the circumstances. "Still, I'm not going to let a little thing like that stop me."

Springing forward, he thudded the top of his head into a pirate bear's bulging belly, winding it. He flipped himself up and over the bear, before kicking him on the back of the head on the way down.

Sir Hopsalot landed in a circle of enemies and winked one of his glassy eyes. "Now, which of you chaps wants to go next?"

The ray guns, cutlasses and custard pies all took aim.

"Kiss your foot goodbye, do-gooder!" one of the soldier-bears snarled.

Vernon yelped. "Lisa Marie, if you've got a plan, now would be a good time to use it!"

Lisa Marie finished tapping the screen with one final firm prod. She looked up as the invading bears suddenly went rigid, their eyes widening as their mouths fell open. Vernon and Bearvis both got to their feet, watching as soldiers, pirates, clowns and elephant began to vibrate.

"What's happening?" Vernon asked.

Lisa Marie angled the phone screen so he could see it. The display was filled with hundreds of emojis, many of them poop-related.

"I'm flooding their control chips," Lisa Marie announced. "It should slow them down."

There was a series of loud bangs, and the air was suddenly full of fluff and fur.

"Or it might make their heads explode," she concluded. She smiled awkwardly at Vernon and the others. "Whoops!"

"Okay, so that works," said Vernon. "Will it have blown up all of them?"

Lisa Marie shook her head. "Doubt it. Only those who were close by."

"Still, jolly impressive, what!" said Sir Hopsalot. He bowed. At least, Lisa Marie guessed that was what he was doing, but it was hard to be sure. "I appreciate your assistance, my dear, but I assure you I had it all in hand."

He glanced down at himself again. "Well, not in *hand*, exactly, but under control."

"Can we use the Wi-Fi to call out?" asked

Vernon. "We can warn people the army is going to come for them."

Lisa Marie shook her head. "It's a local network. It's not connected to the internet."

"Gah!" Vernon groaned.

Bearvis stroked his furry chin thoughtfully. "What I want to know is, how come those guys didn't lose their heads?" he asked, narrowing his eyes at the hench-bears.

"We don't have chips," Cuddlyplump explained.

"Of course. You're probably evil enough already," sniffed Lisa Marie. "Ursine didn't think he'd need to control you."

"We're not evil!" Mr. Fluffton protested. "We don't care about the taking-over-the-world stuff, but if we didn't help Ursine he'd have turned us into stuffed toys again."

"Yeah," agreed Cuddlyplump. "We never really wanted to get involved in any of this world-conquering stuff. We just want to hide in our den, eat candy, play online on the Xbox and chill out."

"Sounds like the perfect Saturday," said Vernon, a little wistfully.

"Wait. How can you play online?" asked Lisa Marie. "It's a local network."

"There's another network," Cuddlyplump said. "Not Wi-Fi, though. We plug into it."

Vernon blinked suddenly and stepped back as an idea hit him. They didn't hit him often, but when they did, they hit him hard.

"Wait. Hold on. I'm thinking of something," he announced.

"That's a first," said Lisa Marie.

"Shhh!" Vernon shushed. He rapped his knuckles against the top of his head, trying to make his brain work faster. "I think . . . Yes. I think I have an idea."

He grabbed the hench-bears and lifted them, one in each hand. "You two are going to take me to your Xbox!"

Lisa Marie rolled her eyes. "You can't seriously be thinking about games at a time like this?"

Vernon looked down at his sister. "Okay, one: I'm always thinking about games," he said. "And two: trust me. I have an idea. I just need you to slow the army down until I come back."

Lisa Marie bit her lip. "I'm not sure we should split up."

"It won't be for long," Vernon assured her. To her surprise, he put his arms around her and hugged her. As he was still holding Mr. Fluffton and Cuddlyplump, they ended up hugging her too. "I won't be far away."

"Have no fear, fair maiden. I, Sir Hopsalot, shall accompany him on his quest!"

He sprang in the direction of the door, his chin held high. "Onward!"

"I'd better go and follow Foothead," said Vernon. He smiled at his little sister, then shot Bearvis a solemn stare. "Look after her."

"You have my word, son," Bearvis drawled.

And then, with a final nod, Vernon raced off after Sir Hopsalot, and before Lisa Marie could say anything else, he was gone.

She took a moment to compose herself, then rolled up her sleeves and unhooked another teddy from its rope. "Okay, Theodore," she said. "Let's try this again."

Ursine Kodiak knelt on the floor, surrounded by circuitboards, lengths of wire and various bits of scrap metal.

His suit was stained with oil and grease. His beard was wilder than ever, from when he'd accidentally electrocuted himself, and he was still suffering the effects of several self-inflicted wedgies.

"Finished," he panted. "It's done."

The digital eye on the screen swiveled down and studied the metal figure towering above Ursine.

It was sort of teddy-bear shaped, but the size of a fully grown adult human. Taller, probably. Wider, definitely. Its shoulders were as broad as a small family car, while its arms were as thick as telephone poles. One of them ended in a hand the size of a trash can lid, while the other didn't have a hand at all. Instead, one of the tanks' cannons had been fixed to the wrist, ready to obliterate anything that got in its way.

"Not bad," Grizz's voice said. "Not bad at all."

On-screen, the eye slowly closed. All around the factory, the lights went dark and the machines fell silent. Ursine's eyes scanned the growing shadows, trying to figure out what this meant.

"Hello?" he whispered.

No reply.

Slowly, Ursine got to his feet. "Uh . . . anyone there?" he asked.

Nothing.

Ursine gave a little cheep of excitement, barely able to believe his luck. Something must've happened to the artificial intelligence software. Maybe Mommy Bear was fighting back. Whatever it was, the nightmare was over.

Turning, he moved to flee, only for an enormous metal hand to clamp down on his shoulder.

Ursine turned just as the robot bear's eyes illuminated in a sinister shade of red.

"And just where do you think you're going?" growled Grizz, his metal jaw snapping up and down. "I still have plans for you, meatbag!"

Vernon couldn't believe quite how big Ursine's underground complex was. After a long, tiring climb up several sets of stairs, he stumbled into a little room, then flopped onto a beanbag that had been set up in front of a TV. As he fell, he landed on top of Cuddlyplump and Mr. Flufftton. They complained about being squashed, but he was too exhausted to move.

Sir Hopsalot hopped over to join him. "What kept you?" he asked. "I've been here for almost five minutes."

"That . . . was a lot . . . of stairs," Vernon wheezed. Eventually, and with a lot of difficulty, he rolled off the beanbag and landed bottom first on a half-eaten pizza.

"Oh man, my ham and pineapple!" Cuddlyplump grumbled. "I was going to eat that later."

Vernon dropped the two hench-bears in the

corner and instructed Sir Hopsalot to watch them while he fired up the Xbox.

"Right you are!" Sir Hopsalot said, glaring at the two tightly bound bears. "These two aren't going anywhere!"

"You'd better not delete our saved games," Mr. Fluffton warned as Vernon added his profile to the console and logged in.

"Don't tempt me," he said. "Do you have a headset?"

"It's over there," said Cuddlyplump, nodding to a stack of Chinese takeout tubs. A wire and part of a headphone poked out from between two silver foil trays.

"Ugh. It's got chow mein on it," Vernon said, wiping the headset on the beanbag.

He pulled it on just as his avatar appeared on-screen, and flicked over to his friends list. "Come on, be online, be online . . . ," he whispered.

Several names popped up as being active and Vernon let out a cheer. "Yes!"

He scrolled to the first active name, Psycho-Gamer88349 and clicked Join Party.

"Where've you been?" Drake demanded through the headset. "You were supposed to be in the tournament."

"Yes, but listen—" Vernon began.

"We got massacred! It was embarrassing."

"I know, but—"

"I'm going to kill you, Vern. We all are," Drake continued. "Me and the lads, we're going to—"

"Will you just shut up?!" Vernon shouted. "You have to listen. This is important."

He fully expected Drake to shout him down, but to Vernon's surprise, he didn't.

"Well, go on, then," Drake spat. "What is it?"

Vernon hesitated. If he told Drake the truth, he'd either ruthlessly mock him or threaten to kill him again; there was no way of telling which. Even if Drake did believe him, he wouldn't help. He wasn't a helping kind of guy, not unless there was something in it for him.

No, this was going to require a different approach. Vernon racked his brains and looked around the room for inspiration. His eyes fell on the three teddy bears.

"Have you heard about the teddy parade?" he said.

Vernon could practically hear Drake frown. "You what?"

"There's a teddy parade today. All these high-tech robot-teddy things are going to be coming to town. It's going to be a big show. There'll probably be music and dancing and stuff."

"Ugh. So?" snapped Drake, sounding

completely disgusted by the whole idea. "Why are you telling me this?"

Vernon took a deep breath. "So, I know how we can ruin it. I know how we can make all the teddy bears' heads explode. My sister and all her friends are really looking forward to it. Imagine how disappointed everyone will be if we ruin it. That'll be fun, right?"

There was silence from the headset for a while. Vernon felt his heart sink. Drake wasn't going to go for it. He wasn't buying it.

Then, out of nowhere: "Go on," said Drake. "I'm listening. . . ."

While Bearvis gathered up the weapons the soldier-bears had dropped, Lisa Marie and Theodore paced back and forth in front of their army. Calling it an army was being generous, Lisa Marie knew, but she felt it was important to try to think positively.

This wasn't easy. Upstairs somewhere, Grizz had assembled a thousand-strong fighting force, equipped with tanks and fighter jets. Down here, Lisa Marie and Theodore Steiffenhume III had cobbled together a group of just thirty teddies, most of whom were missing limbs, eyes or—in one case—a head.

As they walked, Theodore introduced some

of the bears. "You know Jimmy Three Legs and Uncle Noface," he said.

Lisa Marie didn't know them, actually, but she nodded and smiled to suggest she did.

They passed a couple of other bears—one vastly overstuffed, the other just twelve centimeters tall. "Norman and Tiny Norman," Theodore continued.

"Hi, Norman," said Lisa Marie, nodding to the bigger bear.

"No, that's Tiny Norman," Theodore corrected. He indicated the smaller bear. "That's Norman."

"All right?" said Norman in a surprisingly deep voice.

"Uh, but . . . ," Lisa Marie began, then decided not to ask. "Good to meet you both."

The introductions continued. Theodore pointed out Doris the Teeth, Holey Dan, Cousin Upside-Down and Tommy Torso. Another of the bears was introduced as the Twins even though there only appeared to be one of them.

Lisa Marie generally prided herself on being

patient and polite, but now was not the time to be either.

"I'd love to meet everyone, but we're kind of in a rush," she reminded Theodore. "We've got a problem, you see?" she said, addressing the sort-of-army. "An evil teddy is planning to take over the world."

"Why?" asked Norman.

"How's that our problem?" asked Holey Dan.

"What's the world?" asked Cousin Upside-Down.

There was a general unhappy murmuring from the bears, with the exception of Uncle No-face and the headless bear, who both said nothing.

Lisa Marie thought for a moment. "The world is where we live. It's an amazing place, filled with incredible things like . . . like . . . the Great Wall of China, and tropical rain forests, and huge mountain ranges and—"

"Ducks," said Theodore.

Lisa Marie hesitated. "Ducks?"

"Yes." Theodore nodded. "I rather like ducks."

"Okay. And ducks," said Lisa Marie.

"And music, honey," Bearvis chimed in. "Can't forget that."

"Right. And music. But most importantly, it's full of children who love teddy bears," Lisa Marie continued. "Children who *depend* on teddy bears to help them sleep, or to cheer them up, or to make them feel safe when they're afraid. Teddy bears like you."

The murmuring died away. Everyone fell silent. Especially Uncle Noface and the headless bear, who fell twice as silent as everyone else.

Lisa Marie pointed upward. "The bears up there, they want to hurt those children. Or lock them away. I'm not entirely sure, but whatever it is, it won't be good. Not for the kids, and not for their teddies. There'll be no more teddy sleepovers, no more teddy bears picnics, no more *cuddles*."

A series of concerned gasps rose from the group. "No cuddles?" said Doris the Teeth, spraying saliva through her enormous gnashers. "That won't do at all."

"But we can stop them," Lisa Marie said. "You and me. Us. Together. We can stop them."

The bears pulled themselves up to their full heights and proudly puffed out their chests.

"Yeah!"

"Let's do it!"

"We'll show 'em!"

Jimmy Three Legs took one and a half steps forward. "Uh, I have a question. How many of them are there?"

Lisa Marie tried not to let the worry show on her face. "They outnumber us a bit," she admitted.

"Define 'a bit,'" said Jimmy Three Legs.

"There are about a thousand of them," Lisa Marie said.

"What?"

"How many?"

"Forget it!"

"And they have jets and tanks," Theodore added. Lisa Marie shot him a sharp look and he smiled anxiously. "Sorry. I thought I was helping."

"And you want us to stand up to them? That's insane!" cried one of the bears.

"We wouldn't stand a chance," said another.

Bearvis stepped forward. "Hey, now, hold

on there just a second," he said in his distinctive drawl. "Y'all listen, and y'all listen good. This girl here, I saw her take on a whole bunch of monster bears just last night. I'm talking vampires, werewolves, ghosts, aliens . . . these kinda weird ones who were all slimy and disgusting. I don't know what those were, but they were unpleasant. Real unpleasant."

He gave himself a shake.

"Point is, this girl right here, she stopped 'em all. When the odds were stacked against her and the chips were down, she rose to the challenge and she slapped them bad guys so hard they didn't know what hit 'em."

He met Lisa Marie's gaze and smiled. "If anyone can take care of business, it's her. And it's my honor to stand by her side." He punched the air and raised his voice into a rallying cry. "So who's with me?"

No one moved. No one spoke.

Bearvis held his fist in the air until it started to look a bit awkward, and he lowered it again.

"Anyone?" he asked.

There was a shuffling from the Duds. Uncle Noface stumbled forward, his arms reaching blindly ahead of him as he felt his way. A few of the other bears stepped aside, clearing a path for him.

With some difficulty, Noface finally reached Lisa Marie. Hooking an arm around her, he raised a paw and gave a thumbs-up to the rest of the army. Or in what he thought was the right direction, at least.

Bearvis leaned closer to Lisa Marie and whispered. "You think he knows he's facing the wrong way?"

"I don't know. Let's just go with it," Lisa Marie whispered back.

Tiny Norman lumbered over next. He nodded to Bearvis, then wrapped his bulky arms around Lisa Marie and hugged her. "I'm in," he said in a voice that sounded like he'd been inhaling helium.

Cousin Upside-Down came to join them, then Holey Dan. Soon, Lisa Marie was encased in a cocoon of furry bodies as the other teddies rushed over to join the group hug.

"I think we can safely say they're in," said
Theodore.

"You got your army, honey," said Bearvis.
"Now, what's the plan?"

"Vernon said we should slow Grizz's army
down, but I think we can do better than that,"

Lisa Marie said. "We need to get to the central terminal on the factory floor. The screen with the big eye. Once we're there, I can hack Grizz's systems. We're not just going to slow the army down, we're going to stop it!"

"Sounds good. What about us?" Bearvis asked. "The King don't know nothin' about no hacking."

A smile spread slowly across Lisa Marie's face. "You guys are going to be the distraction."

Grizz's metal feet clanked on the concrete floor as he paced back and forth in front of the amassed ranks of his troops. They all stood to attention, ray guns loaded, cutlasses raised, custard pies and lollipop sticks held ready.

The robotic frame that now housed Grizz's artificial intelligence towered above them all, its metal jaw twisted into a cruel mockery of a grin.

"Listen up, furballs," Grizz barked. He pointed his cannon-hand at the long garage-like door behind him. It was rolled up now, revealing a panoramic view of the town below. "You all know your mission. One: we go out there. Two: we destroy everything and round up all the meatbags we find. Three . . ." His smile broadened. "We repeat until the world is ours."

He cast his eyes across the army. "Any questions?"

A paw raised in the third row. Grizz opened fire with his cannon-hand, and the bear became a cloud of burning fluff.

"Any other questions?" he boomed. This time, nobody raised their paw. Red lights blazed in his hollow eye sockets. "Yeah, I thought not," he said. "Now, everyone roll . . ."

A screech of feedback echoed around the complex. All eyes raised to the overhead speakers.

"Ladies and gentlemen," a voice boomed. "Bearvis has entered the building."

A door opened at the far end of the room, revealing a teddy in a sequined outfit standing in a dramatic pose. He had a microphone clutched in one paw, and held it close to his mouth.

"Please, no applause," he said, even though nobody had been clapping. He paced forwards,

addressing the mismatched crowd of bears. "Lookin' good," he said, pointing and winking at a bear in a tutu. The bear giggled a little, then blushed.

"So, you're alive again," said Grizz, raising his cannon-arm. "Don't worry. I can soon change that."

"Not so fast, son," said Bearvis. He twisted his hips and adopted a dramatic stance. "A-one, a-two, a-one-two-three-four," Bearvis boomed, and then he began to sing.

For such a small teddy, Bearvis had a powerful set of lungs. The song he sang was an uptempo rock number about being a "lovin' teddy bear," and many of the bears found their feet tapping along to the beat, which made Grizz furious.

"Don't just stand there watching that idiot. Go get him!"

Three soldiers, two ballerinas and a bear dressed like a Mexican wrestler raced toward Bearvis just as he reached the high notes of the chorus. Before they could pounce on him, Bearvis sidestepped clear and Tiny Norman charged in, using his bulk to scatter the soldier-bears like bowling pins.

"What the . . . ?" Grizz growled. A banshee scream from on high made him look up. Doris the Teeth and Holey Dan burst from the air vents and dropped into the middle of the army. Twelve other bears dropped down behind them, screeching and howling and lashing out with as many limbs as they had available.

"We're under attack!" roared one of the soldiers. He and several others turned to run, only to be blocked by Uncle Noface, Cousin Upside-Down and the bear without a head.

The Duds all raised their paws and waved them ominously, while Cousin Upside-Down let out a low, ghostly moan.

"Arr! Who are these bears?" a pirate bear yelped. "Where they be coming from?"

"And why's that one got no head?" cried a clown bear.

A soldier-bear raised his ray gun. "They'll all have no heads in a minute," he growled.

A blur of sequins slammed into the soldier-bear, flooring him with a spinning karate kick and sending his ray gun clattering across the ground.

"Well, hey now," said Bearvis. "I'm afraid I can't let you do that."

Next door, Lisa Marie positioned herself in front of the computer screen. Theodore stood behind her, shuffling nervously from foot to foot. "You know how to work this contraption, yes?"

Lisa Marie cracked her knuckles and waggled her fingers above the keyboard. "Yes. I think so. I mean, I'm sure I'll work it out," she said.

Theodore gulped. "That does not fill me with confidence."

"Grizz's artificial intelligence is still new, so it's still learning. I can stop it now before it gets too smart." The keys clacked as her fingers flew across them. "Right. So I just need to access the central processing core, then reprogram the primary functions."

She tapped several more keys. With each button she pressed, a frown grew deeper on her face.

"That's weird," she said. "I can't find any trace of him."

Theodore let out a little squeak of excitement. "Did Mommy Bear take back control?"

Lisa Marie jabbed a few more buttons. "No. No, it's like the system has been wiped. Or, no, not wiped. More like—"

"Downloaded," said a voice from behind them.

They turned to find Ursine Kodiak pointing a teddy-bear-sized ray gun at Lisa Marie. "He's no longer in there. He made me build him a body," Ursine said. He tried to smile, then whimpered as he slapped himself in the face. "It wasn't my fault. He implanted me with a control chip, you see? I'm under his command."

His eyes seemed to bulge in fear. He dropped his voice to a whisper. "Red wire. The red wire," he said, staring meaningfully at Lisa Marie. She looked around for a red wire but couldn't see one anywhere.

"What do you mean?" Lisa Marie asked.

"Doesn't matter," Ursine said, his voice a terrified giggle. "Too late. It's too late."

Theodore looked Ursine up and down. "Oh, you must be Him Upstairs. You're the man in charge."

Ursine shook his head. "If only. I'm not in charge anymore. Grizz is the master now. All I can do is follow orders."

As if to prove his point, he poked himself in one eye, then tugged sharply on his beard.

"I'm sorry. I really am. I wanted you to rule the world with me." He gave himself a shake. "Save the world, I mean. I wanted you to *save* the world with me. But my orders are very clear, I'm afraid. I have to stun you and bring you to him." He raised the ray gun. "I really am terribly sorry."

Lisa Marie raised her hands. "No, don't!" she yelped.

"It won't hurt you," Ursine said. "It'll only knock you out."

"I don't want to be knocked out!" Lisa Marie
protested.

Ursine's finger tightened on the trigger. Lisa
Marie screwed her eyes shut and braced herself.

"Poop."

Lisa Marie opened one eye.

"Poop. Poop. Smiley face," said Ursine.

Lisa Marie and Theodore exchanged glances.

"Smiley face, Sassy girl, Sassy girl, poop, poop, thumbs-up, thumbs-up, smiley face."

The words tumbled faster and faster from Ursine's mouth, his eyes widening in panic as he realized he couldn't stop. The gun fell from his grasp and clattered to the floor.

"Pooppooppoopsmileyfacesassygirlsassygirlthumbsuptongueoutpooppoopoo—"

Ursine's whole body went stiff as a board, then toppled backward on to the floor.

"Pooooooooooooooooooooop," he concluded. Then his eyes closed and he began to snore.

Theodore raised his furry eyebrows. "Well now," he muttered. "There's something you don't see every day. Did you do that?"

"It's like someone flooded his control chip," Lisa Marie said. "But it wasn't me."

A metal grate fell out of the wall beside her. Vernon squeezed through the gap, his mobile phone in his hand, a broad grin on his face. "Hey, sis," he said, holding up the phone to show a screen filled with emojis. "You miss me?"

Lisa Marie raced over to Vernon and gave him a hug. "Vernon! It was you! You saved me!"

Vernon accepted the hug at first, but then caught Theodore smiling at them and brushed her away.

"All right, all right, get off," he said.

"So . . . wait. Was the emoji thing your big secret plan?" Lisa Marie asked. "Because if it was, then it was really just my plan from earlier, which you copied."

"No! I mean, yes, I did use your emoji trick just then, but that wasn't where I went earlier," Vernon said. He straightened his back and proudly puffed out his chest. "I found a way to call for help."

Lisa Marie gasped. "You phoned the police?"

Vernon shuffled awkwardly and scratched the back of his head. "Um, not *exactly*. I'll explain later. I left Sir Hopsalot guarding Cuddlyplump and Mr. Fluffton. What's happening up here?"

"I thought I could hack the central processing core and turn Grizz off, but he's not in there anymore," Lisa Marie said. "He's got a body."

Vernon frowned. "What kind of body?"

"Um . . . that kind," said Theodore. He was pointing to the screen, which now showed a towering robo-bear surrounded by soldiers, two lollipop ladies and a little beach bear with a Hawaiian shirt and a surfboard. To Lisa Marie's dismay, Bearvis and the Duds were all kneeling on the floor in front of him, their hands behind their heads.

"Hey there," boomed Grizz's voice through the screen's speakers. "Thanks for sending me all your friends to play with. I had a great time."

"Leave them alone!" Lisa Marie warned.

"I tell you what. I'll make you a deal," said Grizz. "You come through here and give yourself up, and I won't turn them all into balls of stuffing. What do you say?"

Vernon caught Lisa Marie by the arm. "You can't," he said.

Lisa Marie straightened her back and lifted her head. "I have to," she said, and Vernon knew from the look on her face that there was no point trying to argue.

"Don't worry about me," she said. "Go and try to get that help you called to hurry up."

Vernon shook his head. "You're kidding, right? We're going together."

He held a hand out and Lisa Marie took it. Tears sprang to her eyes, but she smiled through them. "Weird couple of days, huh?"

Vernon snorted. "You can say that again."

Theodore took Lisa Marie's other hand. "I'm with you too," he said. "I may not have known you long, but I'm proud to stand by your side."

"Thank you," said Lisa Marie. She took a deep breath; then all three of them crossed the factory floor and passed through the doorway into the next room. Several ray guns, tank turrets, custard pies and missiles all took aim at them as they walked toward the robotic Grizz and his helpless hostages.

Bearvis nodded sadly at Lisa Marie, and she felt guilty that he seemed to be apologizing. This wasn't his fault. This was nobody's fault but her own. She should never have sent Bearvis and the others into danger. How could she have been so stupid?

"Okay, we're here," said Lisa Marie. "Now let them go."

"I will," Grizz agreed. "Just as soon as I've chipped them all and placed them under my control."

"What? No! That wasn't the deal," Lisa Marie cried.

"Deal? There was no 'deal,' meatbag!" Grizz snarled. "I'm in charge here. I make the decisions. I've *won*. I'm going to chip these bears, and then you're going to watch as we roll down the hill and first take over your meatbag town, then your meatbag country, then the whole meatbag—"

Beside him, a teddy bear's head went *bang,* showering him in fluff and fragments of fur.

A whole row of teddies behind him went next, each of their heads bursting open until clumps of fluff filled the air like tiny clouds.

"What is this?" Grizz demanded.

"Oh man, they came," Vernon whispered. "They actually came!"

Bang! B-Bang, bang! More soldier-teddies exploded. From over by the doorway, there came a sharp cackle of glee. Drake and a group of other boys raced in through the open doorway, frantically tapping at their phone screens.

"You were right, Vern!" Drake bellowed. Behind him, his cronies cheered as a couple of clown teds and a ballerina bear lost their heads. "This is awesome!"

Lisa Marie gasped. "You convinced Drake to help us?"

Vernon smirked. "Well, not *exactly,* but more or less. I gave them the Wi-Fi code for the private network here and told them exactly how they could spoil a teddy bear parade. The rest just took care of itself."

"You're a genius!" Lisa Marie told him.

"Stop them!" bellowed Grizz, but most of the soldiers were twitching and spasming now as their control chips were flooded with emojis.

"Ladies and gentlemen, let's take care of business," Bearvis commanded. As one, the Duds pounced on the closest soldiers, wrestling their weapons away and knocking them to the ground.

Bearvis launched a flying kick at Grizz, but an enormous robotic hand swatted him to the floor.

"You three have done it again!" Grizz roared. "Why can't you just let me win?" He growled at them, his robotic face twisting in rage. "Well, it's not over yet!"

There was a flash from the robo-bear's feet and Grizz rose unsteadily into the air on a cushion of fire, forcing Bearvis and the other teddies to scatter.

"I don't need them. I don't need anyone!" Grizz bellowed. "I can take out the town all by myself. Just you watch me!"

He rocketed upward, his dense metal body punching a hole right through the roof. Lisa Marie and Vernon raced through the sea of exploding soldier-bears until they found Bearvis.

"He's escaping. What do we do?" Vernon yelped.

Lisa Marie looked around, searching for something—anything—that might help. Her eyes fell on one of the fighter jets. They were teddy-bear-sized, but the teddies they'd been built for were almost as big as she was. It would be a squeeze, but there was no other choice.

"Vernon, stay here and make sure none of

Grizz's bears escape," she said, racing toward the planes. "Bearvis, come with me."

"Where are you going?" asked Vernon.

"Where we always go," said Lisa Marie, throwing open a jet's canopy and clambering inside. "To save the day!"

19

Bearvis sat behind the controls, staring at them with a look on his face that suggested he had no idea what any of them did. This was a bit worrying, as they had already taken off and were now flying straight for one of the bunker's solid concrete walls.

"Turn!" Lisa Marie cried. She was wedged into the seat behind him, her knees tucked under her chin.

"Sure thing, honey," Bearvis drawled. "Uh, any idea how?"

"The control-pad thing!"

"This control-pad thing?"

"It's the only control-pad thing there!" Lisa Marie squealed.

Bearvis jerked the little stick on the control pad and the jet banked sharply to the right. Everyone in the bunker who hadn't already been blown to pieces by emojis screamed and threw themselves to the floor as the plane roared above them, its thrusters spewing flames, its sleek wings slicing through the air.

The jet tilted. Sparks sprayed as the tip of one wing scraped the doorframe, and then it rocketed out of the bunker and Lisa Marie shivered in the sudden cold of the world outside.

"Do you see him?" she cried, searching the sky.

"It's a big old airspace, honey," Bearvis said. "Finding him is gonna be like finding a needle in a . . . No, wait. There he is."

He pointed to where a large metal teddy bear was racing through the sky with flames billowing from his feet.

"That was actually a whole lot easier than I

thought," Bearvis said. "I mean, it's kinda hard to miss him."

"He's heading for town. We have to stop him!" said Lisa Marie, then covered her head with her hands as a missile screamed past them.

Bearvis glanced over his shoulder. "Uh-oh. We got incoming."

Lisa Marie looked back to see another jet chasing them. A bear dressed like a cowboy was in the pilot's seat, his hat pulled low on his head.

He opened fire with another tiny missile, forcing Bearvis to swing the plane out of its path.

"More of them, look!" Lisa Marie said as two more planes flew out of the bunker.

"Aw, man, that ain't good," said Bearvis. He sent the jet into a dive, then pulled up sharply, avoiding another missile. "I can't dodge these guys forever."

A voice crackled from the control console. "Don't worry. I've got them."

Lisa Marie gasped. "Vernon? Is that you?"

She looked back just as one of the chasing jets went into a spin and crashed into the hillside. Another plane appeared behind it, slicing gracefully through the sky. To Lisa Marie's surprise, the cockpit was empty.

"Turns out you can take the control pads off and fly them remotely," Vernon's voice continued. "It's just like playing *Battle War Two*!"

There was a *bang* as another of the pursuing jets crashed.

"I've got these guys," Vernon said. "Go and stop Grizz!"

Lisa Marie gave Bearvis a squeeze on the shoulder. "You heard him. Let's go and stop that robo-bear!"

"Ten-four, honey!" He jammed the control stick to the right and the jet swung around until it was directly behind Grizz. "We're on his tail, little darlin'!" Bearvis announced. "Now what? Shoot him with missiles?"

"No," said Lisa Marie, shouting to make herself heard over the roaring of the wind. "It's too dangerous. We might miss and hit the town."

"I guess we could crash into him," Bearvis said. He winced. "Though that's probably gonna hurt us more than it hurts him."

"Get closer. I have an idea," Lisa Marie said.

"Sorry, honey, I don't know if this hunka junk can go any faster."

"Sure it can." Lisa Marie leaned over and pressed a button marked AFTERBURNERS. "This should do the job," she said.

Or rather, that's what she tried to say. What she actually said was "This should WAAAAAAAAAAAA AAAAAAAAAAAARGH!" as a pulsing blue

181

flame ignited behind the jet and launched it screaming through the sky.

In a second, they had halfway closed the gap on the robo-Grizz. Bearvis wrestled with the controls, steering the jet toward the rocketing robo-bear.

"We're almost on him, little darlin,'" Bearvis said. "You want me to smash into him and see what happens?"

"No," said Lisa Marie. "Just get us as close as you can."

"That ain't gonna be a problem," Bearvis told her. The afterburner was hurtling them in Grizz's direction at incredible speed. Any second now, they'd shoot right over the top of him.

Lisa Marie realized she had no time to lose. She didn't know what she was going to do, exactly, but she had to do *something* and do it now. Her body began moving before her brain had come up with a plan. Unsquashing herself from the airplane's seat, she scrambled to her feet, briefly wondered if she'd lost her mind and then jumped.

Distance-wise, the jump wasn't all that

impressive. She traveled just a couple of yards, most of them in a downward direction. The fact that she was jumping from a moving plane onto a flying robot earned her a whole lot of style points, though.

She landed on Grizz's back, slid sideways and frantically grasped for a handhold. She gave a yelp of triumph as her fingers dug beneath a sheet of armor plating and she jerked to a stop, her legs dangling over the long drop to the ground far below.

Bearvis and the jet screamed on, swooping low over the town and almost crashing into the church spire.

"Have you lost your stuffing, kid?" Grizz barked. "You must be out of your mind!"

He was right, Lisa Marie knew. This was crazy. What had she been thinking? It didn't make sense. She was usually so . . . so *sensible*.

"Um, maybe," she admitted. "Let me get back to you on that one."

Kicking and scrabbling, she pulled herself up onto Grizz's back. His head rotated like an owl's until it was pointing backward. His metal jaw was curved into a wide grin. "And here I was worried I wouldn't get a chance to personally destroy you," he said. "Guess I didn't need to worry."

Lisa Marie's mind raced. Why had she jumped? There had to be a reason. She was a logical sort of girl. Jumping out of a jet onto an evil robo-bear was all very exciting, but it wasn't *her*. It wasn't something she would do. Not without good reason.

Why had she jumped? What niggling idea at the back of her brain had made her leap from the plane?

Grizz raised an arm. The metal hand began to spin, the fingers becoming twirling blades. "Say goodbye, meatbag!"

And that was when Lisa Marie saw it . . . sticking out of Grizz's back and flapping wildly in the roaring wind. It was why she had jumped. It was the thing her subconscious had guessed would be waiting for her.

It was a red wire. The red wire Ursine had mentioned.

Lisa Marie grabbed it with both hands and

tugged. Once. Twice. Grizz's voice became a slur of nonsense words as his metal features twitched and jerked. His hand stopped spinning. His jets stopped firing.

"Whzzzzt hvvvvvk yooooooouuuoooo dnnn?" he demanded.

And then gravity caught hold of him and they both began to fall.

They were halfway to the ground when Lisa

Marie heard the jet engine. Three-quarters of the way when she saw the shadow pass above them.

The furry hand caught her by the ankle just five or six yards from the ground. Looking up, she saw Bearvis hanging out of the upside-down jet, his beautiful hair blowing back in the breeze.

The plane spun so it was facing right-side up again. Lisa Marie flopped into the seat directly behind Bearvis.

"I got you, honey," he told her. "Ain't no one gonna hurt you now."

The plane thudded against the hillside, tossing Lisa Marie and Bearvis into the air. They both screamed as they flew up, up, up, then continued screaming as they fell down, down, down.

They landed with a series of *oof*s and *ooyah*s, then lay on the grass for a while, trying to figure out if they were still alive and, if so, how many pieces they were in.

After almost a full minute of thinking about it, Lisa Marie was still unable to decide. "Did we survive?" she asked.

"I'm gonna have to get back to you on that

one, little darlin,'" Bearvis told her. "The jury's still out."

They both sat up. They both groaned. They both clutched their heads.

"That still qualifies as a rescue, right?" Bearvis asked.

He gestured to a smoking crater in the ground a little farther up the hillside. "I mean, we're in better shape than that guy."

They picked their way up the hill, kicking through the debris and chunks of scorched metal. They finally found Grizz's head wedged between two rocks, a dim red light glowing in his eye sockets.

"Careful now, honey," Bearvis warned as Lisa Marie picked the head up. He adopted a karate stance, ready to leap into action if the robot head tried any funny business.

"I think we're safe," Lisa Marie said. Then she screamed as the mouth snapped open and the eyes blazed.

"Think again, meatbag!" Grizz snarled. His voice sounded flat and crackled badly as he spoke. "You haven't heard the last of me. You hear me? You haven't heard-d-d-d-d-d-d-d-dddddddddddddd . . ."

The voice became a low, continuous tone, and then both it and the light in Grizz's eyes faded away completely.

"Meh. I think we have," said Lisa Marie. She tossed the robotic skull backward over her shoulder, dusted herself off, then turned to Bearvis. "So!" she said. "That was interesting."

"You can say that again," Bearvis agreed. Blue lights flashed down in the town. They could hear sirens. They were distant now but getting closer.

"Lisa Marie!" wheezed Vernon, running down the hillside behind them. "You're okay! Where's Grizz?"

"He's there," said Lisa Marie. "And there. And there's quite a lot of him over there."

"He's gone?" Vernon gasped.

Lisa Marie nodded quite proudly. Not *too* proudly, though, because she didn't like to boast. "What about the soldier-bears?"

"Taken care of," said Vernon. "Drake and the guys blew most of them up. The Duds took care of the rest." He grinned. "Looks like we saved the world."

"Again," said Lisa Marie.

The girl, the boy and the bear all looked down the hill in the direction of the sirens. "I think we're going to have a lot of explaining to do," said Vernon.

Lisa Marie shrugged. "It's nothing we can't handle."

"Aren't you worried about Bearvis being taken away and dissected?"

Bearvis blinked. "Aw, man. I *wasn't* worried about that, but now I am."

Lisa Marie reached down and took Bearvis's paw. She had stopped an army. *Two* armies, in fact.

She set her shoulders, raised her head and gritted her teeth. "I'd like to see them try!"

EPILOGUE

Ursine Kodiak sat up. He tried to remember what was going on, but thinking made his head hurt.

He remembered something about poop. A lot of poop. And smiling.

But mostly poop.

He could hear sirens in the distance. There was laughter, too. Children, he thought. It was harsh, cruel laughter that reminded him of his own childhood and the bullies who used to taunt him.

He felt his heart race at the very thought of them and took a moment to compose himself. He was a grown man now. The bullies were gone. He was a grown man with his own free will and no one could make him do anything he didn't want to—

THWACK.

Ursine slapped himself across the face. There was a sound somewhere deep inside his brain like a computer powering up, and he felt the control chip briefly vibrate.

"Well, well, well," growled a voice in Ursine's head. "You're just the meatbag I've been looking for. . . ."

THE BATTLE OF TEDDY BEARS CONTINUES!

ABOUT THE AUTHOR

Barry Hutchison was born and raised in the Highlands of Scotland. He was just eight years old when he decided he wanted to become a writer and seventeen when he sold his first piece of work. In addition to the Night of the Living Ted series, he is the author of the Invisible Fiends series and *The Shark-Headed Bear Thing*. He also writes for TV. Barry lives in Fort William, Scotland, with his partner and their two children.

ABOUT THE ILLUSTRATOR

Lee Cosgrove has been doodling for as long as he can remember. He doodled in his schoolbooks and now he is doodling in children's books. He's probably doodling right now while you're reading this! Lee lives with his wife and two children in Cheshire, England.